K.J. Backer grew up on a tree farm in rural Oregon before moving to the Big Sky State in 1996. She credits her close family bonds, wild imagination, animal affection, and love for books to her humble, country upbringing.

K.J. Backer "retired" from teaching high school history to pursue her dream of writing after adopting her daughter in 2017. (Learn more about her fantasy trilogy, *Nav'Aria* at kjbacker.com.)

She lives in Montana with her amazing husband, wonderful daughter, two adorable pomeranians, handsome tortoise, and HYPER chihuahua.

Written by K.J. Backer
Cover Design and Paw Print Illustrations by Josh Wirth
Edited by Heather Peers
Formatted by Keil Backer
Proofread by Dave Jones

Visit author website at **kjbacker.com** to learn more.

Printed in the United States of America

First Edition: September 2022

ISBN-13: 978-1-7329206-6-8

The Legend of

Tiny Tails

K.J. Backer

Be Brave!

KJBah.

For Diana, the loveliest and most
supportive Mama & G-Ma out there

And for my darling kids:
Jarica, Drogo, Nala, Kublai, and Drax

PROLOGUE

"No way! There is no way that happened. You're an idiot if you fell for that," Rowen teased, sauntering off with his chihuahua puppy pack. Their tails wagging in unison as they left the runt of their litter behind.

Thinking himself alone, tears pooled in Duke's large eyes from his bully's taunts.

It was a perfect spring day in Eastern Montana. Not a cloud in the sky, and thankfully, no snow. The warm April breeze scattered fuzzy dandelion seeds and carried the scent of sage grass and wheat. Fat bumblebees feasted on nectar from the nearby rose garden. Robins chirped from rooftops and fences. Chickadees, finches, and swallows gossiped and sang at the feeders, giggling as they splashed around the bird baths, scaring off the smaller western bluebirds. The day was too perfect for tears, I thought, having heard the unkind exchange from the other side of the fence.

"Now wait just a moment," I croaked, surprising the puppy as much as myself. It had been sometime since I'd spoken aloud.

Duke's head snapped up, looking around, and sniffing hurriedly. Most likely thinking one of his wretched siblings had caught him crying.

I cleared my throat as much to get his attention as to warm up my unused vocal cords for the talk. It had been a long, long time.

"W-who's there?" Duke whispered.

Leaning forward, I shoved my head in between the fence panels, to peer at the pup.

The puppy's eyes widened, and he took an involuntary step back. "W-what are you?" Though still nervous, his tone sounded more curious.

"Why, I'm a tortoise, of course," I replied. "My name is Pharaoh. Pleased to meet you, neighbor."

The chihuahua puppy only hesitated for a moment, looking back to see his siblings chasing one another through the yard on the far side. His brother and two sisters were always playing games without him, I knew. I'd heard many similar exchanges over the past few days.

Why did I speak up today?

Something they'd said had sparked a memory in me. One I had long thought buried. It had been many years ago. Best to leave it behind me. But then those voices had teased it... uncovering a section of my memory, and the pitiful puppy's tears had prickled at my stony heart.

A warm, wet tongue licked my scaly cheek, startling an old man from his thoughts.

"I'm Duke," the puppy said after his kind greeting, and then began to hiccup.

Just a tot, I smiled, thinking how long it had been since I'd been given a kiss. *Ah, it's not so bad*, I recollected. *I love Destiny and Mom more than anything, but... animal friends are... well, there's nothing like them.*

"Now, tell me what brought this on. What story does your brother say is untrue?"

Duke cocked his head, sniffling, the sunlight bringing out the shimmer of his blue coat as one of his ears flopped down. My heart melted. *Just a tot indeed.*

"It wasn't just a story," Duke exclaimed, "it's a legend. A real one!"

"Ah, and what is this grand legend?" I inquired, closing my eyes for a moment to soak in the warm rays, enjoying the exuberance in the puppy's voice.

"A bunch of tiny dogs—like me!—defeated an evil owl and coyotes and saved the world. It happened in Montana," though he paused, leaning in, and whispered, "But I don't know what 'Montana' is."

By then my eyes had popped open, and I didn't know whether to laugh or cry. "That sounds like quite the adventure," I murmured.

Duke blurted, "So, you believe me?"

I added, "Well, it wasn't the world. Not really. More like just one girl."

The puppy squeaked and leaped, quivering with excitement, "It's true then? I was right?"

"You were right," I smiled and chuckled as the puppy jumped up. His tiny paws rested on the fence and my shell—to give me another lick on the cheek, his tail wagging faster than before.

"Where did you hear it?"

Duke looked down suddenly as if embarrassed, "I—well, I heard some mourning doves talking about it on the fence the other day. They didn't know I was listening, and I didn't hear all of it. But that's why my brother doesn't believe me. He says they're 'fluff brains.'"

I smiled looking toward P'Jean and Marie, the dove pair, fattening themselves on the cylindrical feeder they so often frequented. I whispered, "Your brother—though 'fluff brain' is an astute description of our bird friends—is wrong. What they shared was true... or at least, mostly true."

"Really? But how do you know, Pharaoh?"

"Well dear one, that's easy. I was there, of course."

"You were there?" The puppy's eyes pleaded as his tiny tail wagged to and fro excitedly. "You have to tell me. Please tell me, Pharaoh. Will you? Will you?"

The puppy's curiosity ignited something in me. "You know, little one, I think I will," I replied, clearing my throat. "Just after I get something to drink."

I knew what I wanted to say. The truth is, I'd held on to this story for far too long. It needed to be shared. It wasn't a story to keep to myself, I now realized. Taking a deep breath, having quenched my thirst, I began.

"There are a few things you should know going into this story. One: My part is only a small one. Two: This is a long story. And three: This isn't a fairytale.

Some of what I'm about to tell you might scare you. But let me assure you, it's a happy story... eventually. It's a story of adventure. Humor. Fun. And suspense. Most of all, it is a story of love. Family love. This is the story of my family, and it is my great honor to share it. I only ask that you save your questions until the end. Alright?"

Duke, trembling with anticipation laid down in the warm grass, the late morning sunshine growing more and more delightful. The fence shadows danced along the yard, and my shell soaked in the blissful spring heat. By now, we'd gained the attention of a few songbirds who chirped happily—within hearing—upon the nearby Maple tree. I nodded at them in greeting. With that, I told the story I'd kept inside for the past fifty years. I told them "The Legend of Tiny Tails."

CHAPTER 1

Caesar leapt off the couch, as the front door closed. *Mom's home! I missed you, Mom!* The black pomeranian buzzed over to kiss and lick every portion of her face as she squatted down to pet him. Suddenly, he froze amidst his frenzied kisses, pausing on one particular scent: Canine.

Who is that? He wondered to himself.

Caesar backed up his tiny four-pound body to get a better look at his mom. Something was up. *What is it, Mom? Where's Dad?*

"Hi Caesar," she said, talking to him as she always did, though never seeming to understand him. He would bark and bark and she would tilt her head quizzically trying to guess what he was saying. Things would be so much easier if humans could speak 'dog.'

Continuing she said, "Now Caesar, Daddy and I have something we want to tell you. You're gonna be a big brother, okay? We felt bad that you're home all day alone while we're at work, so we got you a friend. You need to be nice to her and show her the ropes, alright?"

Caesar bounced up and down. *A sister? A friend? What does this mean? What if I don't like her? Can I think about it? What if she's—*

Before he had time to consider what this might mean for their family of three, in walked Dad holding a tiny bundle. A little black nose poked out of the pink blanket and sniffed audibly.

Caesar could hardly breathe. *Wait? She's already here. You're just springing this on me? No time to consider?*

He paced nervously as Dad walked over and set the bundle down. Out tottered a tiny fluff of white, brown, and black. The Pomeranian puppy trembled slightly but rose to look around. When her eyes met Caesar's, his heart warmed.

He walked to her slowly. She backed up nervously, unsure of his intentions. He smiled and gave her a quick kiss on the cheek and nuzzle, breathing in her scent. *Sister!*

"Awww, see Alex. I knew Caesar would love her too," Mom cooed, bending down to rub behind Caesar's ears.

"I stand corrected… again," Dad mused, adding, "I'll go get dinner going."

He smiled at the pups and kissed his wife before disappearing into the kitchen.

Mom squatted down, "You're a good boy, buddy. This is Empress. You need to look out for her, okay? That's what siblings do."

Caesar leaned into her palm; he loved a good ear scratch. The puppy was sniffing and rolling on her blanket, making all sorts of adorable sniffs and snorts.

Mom laughed. Maybe it would be fun to have a sister around, Caesar mused. He did get awfully lonely during the day… and scared too. This might be great.

"Hey Davina, do you want leftover lasagna or chicken salad?"

Mom murmured, "Be good in here. I'll be right back," to Caesar, still eyeing the puppy, as she went to join Dad.

Their busy work schedules kept them away a lot, and they usually ate leftovers all week. Caesar was used to it. Mom and Dad would cook on Sundays and their meals would last for days. He'd long grown accustomed to all the smells. He yearned to taste some of their human food instead of his boring dog food. Every once in a while, Dad would sneak him something when Mom wasn't looking. He smiled inwardly. This would be great. He would teach Empress all that he knew. Starting with—

He looked over to see her lying in his bed! "Hey, now first thing's first," he lectured, "that's my bed. You'll have to find your own."

She tilted her head at him only briefly, sniffed, and then settled in.

That was the first moment Caesar realized that having a little sister meant sharing. And that didn't sound all that fun.

CHAPTER 2

"Caesar, come on! They're here! They're here," Empress called, bouncing up and down at the door.

It had taken very little time before a fast friendship had developed. Caesar, though he had loved having Mom and Dad to himself, really did enjoy the company during the day. He and Empress had a lot of fun. Sunbathing, playing tug-of-war, seeing who could spin and catch their tail the fastest, scaring the mailman. All sorts of things over the last couple of years. But today was different.

Before Mom left to go teach at the college, where she lectured on Ancient World History and Native American Studies, she had commented, "Be good.

You're gonna be in for a surprise when we get home. We have a new friend for you."

Caesar had been anxious the entire day, barely able to stomach his breakfast. He had only just gotten used to Empress. *Another friend? What did this mean?*

Gravel crunched as the car pulled up outside. Being this far out in the country, one could literally hear a car from a mile or more away.

This was it. Something was coming and going to change their lives forever. Caesar looked forlornly at his favorite toy resting on his bed. Would the next playmate take his toys too? He'd already lost his bed to Empress.

The key twisted in the lock, and before Empress or Caesar could react, a large, shelled creature appeared being rolled through the door on a cart. Caesar gaped as Mom carefully helped slide the creature off onto the floor in front of them.

Mom squatted down grinning widely. "Hey guys, this is Pharaoh. Your new friend."

Empress pressed her body against Caesar's, whispering, "What the heck is that?"

Caesar didn't know. Though he was older, he was as sheltered as she was. He had never seen a creature like this before. Preferring to use the potty pad near the door, he'd hardly ever been outside. Though, knowing as big brother it was his responsibility to go first, he took a couple hesitant steps.

Since Mom seemed happy, it must not be a threat. At least, not yet.

Nervously, he leaned forward. Sniff. Sniff. Sniff. "Hmmmm," he murmured, pondering.

Empress whispered again, "What is it, Caesar? Did she get us a pet rock?"

It hadn't moved yet. Caesar couldn't tell which part of it was the head or the tail. *Was it a rock?* He sniffed further.

"Ahh, what's it doing?" Empress squeaked, quivering, and bouncing up and down.

Caesar stepped back, a small growl escaping his throat.

"No," Mom said in a calm but stern voice. "Now listen here, guys. This is a tortoise. He's different from you, but that's what makes life so wonderful. We're all unique. You're going to have some fun adventures around here. Just give him a chance."

Caesar and Empress skirted around the creature whose head was emerging from the stone-like body. Caesar placed his tiny paws on Mom's bent knees. She knelt down further and scratched behind both his and Empress's ears as they took turns licking her face.

Mom laughed, and the sound made Caesar's heart fill with joy. No matter what, Mom always made him feel better. Though Caesar wished she'd quit coming home with all these surprise friends. *It was a lot to take in! And where was Dad?*

Mom reached her hand out and rubbed it over the creature's *shell*, as she called it. It wasn't fur like his, but the creature—Pharaoh—seemed to respond to her touch. His head tilted upwards. When their eyes met, Caesar dropped back down to all fours and cautiously approached Pharaoh. The pomeranian tentatively sniffed the creature, who tucked back its head immediately at the inspection.

"Shh, no, it's okay," Caesar heard himself whispering. "I won't hurt you." Though as he said it, he wondered if he even could. Pharaoh was way bigger than him, and he really did look like a rock.

Slowly, the tortoise's head began to creep back out from its shell. "Y-y-you promise?"

And for the second time in Caesar's short life, his heart warmed toward another animal sibling. Empress had changed everything about his life, but she'd also brought so much fun and joy. Maybe Pharaoh would do the same.

"I promise. We're brothers now," Caesar said warmly and then turned to eye Empress.

She sniffed and turned back to licking Mom, as she often did when she disagreed with Caesar, choosing to ignore him.

"Empress," Caesar admonished.

"Oh, all right," she sighed, jumping down from Mom, who was praising them for being so adorable.

Pharaoh looked to Caesar as Empress approached.

Caesar nodded at him and whispered encouragingly.

Empress came closer and sniffed.

"Hello," the tortoise whispered. It's voice low but timid. It must have pulled on Empress's heartstrings too, because before long she laid down beside the tortoise, who began nuzzling into her fur.

"I have to get my camera," Mom cooed, yelling for Dad to come look.

He'd, as per usual, disappeared pretty quickly into the kitchen. He loved the pets, Caesar knew, but it was Mom who was their main caretaker.

Caesar smiled watching Mom buzzing around, oohing and snapping pics on her phone. Dad leaned out from the kitchen yelling, "Way to go, pups," between a mouthful of roast beef sandwich.

Empress gushed to tell Pharaoh all the things she

was going to teach him.

Caesar crept quietly away and snuggled in for a quick nap on his favorite dog bed while his sister was occupied. *This is the life*, he sighed, smiling.

CHAPTER 3

"I don't know you guys, this seems pretty dangerous," Empress stated nervously.

Mom had started letting them play outside only recently, saying as long as they stayed close to the house it was alright. She said the fresh air and sunshine was good for Pharaoh. Mom and Dad had built a fenced yard that stretched almost an acre. Lots of grass and rocks and wildflowers as far as the eye could see... aspen and pine trees dotted the area under the expansive blue sky.

Caesar turned back to see Empress teetering on top of the big rock he'd just leapt off. Caesar loved jumping from rock to rock, pretending the ground was hot lava. Empress had loved the game too, but lately she seemed more and more hesitant.

He turned back to her. She was squinting her eyes and seemed to be really focusing. "What is it, Empress?" he asked returning to her and sniffing her face.

"I—I can't really see that much. It's scary up here. Can you see where you're going?"

Caesar felt his stomach grow tense. He could see everything perfectly. There wasn't a patch of shade or cloud to be found on this hot, sunny afternoon.

"What do you mean you can't see? Can you see me right here in front of you?"

She tilted her head, her nose working in overdrive, searching for his scent. She faced him, but he noticed for the first time that her eyes weren't meeting his.

"I don't know," she whispered, trembling.

"Ah, Empress," Caesar whispered, coming closer and nuzzling her cheek. He could smell her fear. She wasn't faking it. Empress had lost her vision.

Pharaoh ambled up to them, a dandelion hanging out from the side of his mouth. Chomping the rest of it, he mumbled, "What's going on? I thought you were taking me to see the creek?"

The "creek" was the rock fountain Mom and Dad

had added so that they could all get water and Pharaoh could soak in the shallows if desired. Apparently, that was also good for tortoises, even though Caesar thought it sounded downright terrible. He hated getting wet! Bath days were the worst!

Empress sat on the rock, unsure of how to get down. She searched for Pharaoh.

"I don't think Empress can see anymore," Caesar responded, knowing there was no way to sugar-coat the truth. "How long has this been going on, Empress?"

She sniffed, a small tear leaking out. "I-I don't know. A week maybe? Or a month? Well, it has seemed pretty dark in the house. I thought it was just from the winter but now..." she hesitated. "Now it's spring and I still can't see. I'm bliiiiind," she wailed.

"Oh, hush," Caesar murmured and jumped to stand beside her on the rock. "It'll be okay. But we need to tell Mom."

While Empress cried, Caesar whispered to Pharaoh, "I think the creek will have to wait."

"I agree. Let's get her inside," Pharaoh murmured.

Caesar sensed a depth to Pharaoh. It made Caesar proud. His brother was a wise reptile.

"It's gonna be alright, Empress. Here, can you

smell me? Grab my tail, okay? I'll lead you back in."

Still sniffing, Empress did as she was told, lightly taking some of his tail in her mouth as he helped her hop down from the rock and head for the back door that Mom had left ajar. Pharaoh walked at her side, reassuring her the entire time.

Together the three friends, furred and shelled, made it back to the safety of the indoors. Mom must have seen it, for the next day, Empress was taken to the vet where they confirmed her condition. She had gone blind from a sudden acquired retinal degeneration syndrome known as SARDS. She was otherwise healthy but would need support as she got used to relying on her other senses.

CHAPTER 4

Another two years passed, and the trio fell into a familiar rhythm. Caesar and Empress would stand at the door wagging their tails goodbye as Mom and Dad left for work each day. Pharaoh would amble over from his earthen habitat that had taken over the once dining room, after munching his grass, weeds, and veggies, and then retire in the afternoon to bask under his heat lamp. They'd talk from time to time. Play games here or there. And snooze most of the day until Mom and Dad returned. They had a cozy home, plenty of water and food, and great company. It was a familiar, easy life.

"What more could three pets want?" Caesar had

commented one day upon hearing Empress complaining to Pharaoh.

"Oh, I don't know," she said. "I guess I'm just dreaming of adventure... like the stories Mom tells."

"But, Empress, you're blind. You don't even like going outside with us anymore."

Empress's lip trembled and her eyes grew glassy.

Caesar sighed, internally kicking himself. That hadn't come out very nice. Not like he'd intended. "Empress, I'm sorry," he began, but she cut him off.

"I know," she stated softly. "I—well—I can still want adventure even if I don't have it anymore. I know with my condition it's not safe for me out there, because I could get lost or hurt. It's better if I just stay inside here. Safe. In my prison."

"Prison?" Caesar exclaimed. "Empress, that's not really what you think of life with us, is it?"

But before she could answer, the lock sounded, and the door swung open to reveal Mom.

Mom? She's home early, Caesar thought. *Her classes usually went long on Tuesdays.* He really did his best to keep track. He made mental notes during dinner when Mom reminded Dad of the next day's schedule. And he specifically remembered Mom had—*Wait,* he paused, reminding himself, *she hadn't said anything.* She'd just eaten quietly last night.

Why hadn't he paid closer attention? Something was going on.

Sniff. Sniff. Sniff. Sniiiiiiiiiiiiff. His nose twitched. Something foreign. Different.

"What is that scent?" He asked, looking to see Empress's nose scrunching and joining in.

Pharaoh stretched out his neck, peering toward Mom.

Caesar stepped toward her hesitantly. Something was definitely going on; he was sure of it. Mom looked... nervous? And happy at the same time. How could that be?

"Hey, guys. I have someone I'd like for you to meet," Mom greeted, and then from behind her stepped into view a child. A human child.

Caesar looked from the girl to his mom in question. *Oh, not again! Mom, who is she? Is she a student? How long is she staying?* Caesar barked.

"Caesar, hush. Don't scare her," Mom said, looking at him sternly before turning toward the girl.

"Go on, sweetheart, it's alright. You can say hi to them. This is Caesar, I told you about him in the car. And over there is Empress. She might be a little hesitant at first since she can't see you. And the handsome tort behind her is Pharaoh."

The girl, Caesar observed, was tan like Mom and

had dark choppy hair with purple streaks in it. She was smaller than Mom but larger than an infant. Caesar guessed she was one of those "tweens" he'd heard of. *Much easier to tell with dogs*, he thought to himself, continuing his inspection of her. Her wrists were covered in black metal bands and beads. Her clothes were black and stunk like sweat. Her jeans had holes all over, as did her sneakers. Her fingernails were painted in chipped green polish, and he could smell dirt under them.

Empress came closer, whispering, "What is it? It stinks."

Caesar grumbled for her to be quiet.

As the girl approached, she bent down and scratched them both behind the ears. *That was a surprise*, Caesar thought. She didn't necessarily look friendly. Probably because he couldn't see her eyes with her bangs hanging over them, but she *felt* alright. She didn't smell mean... just very much in need of a bath.

"Hi," she whispered softly, before wiping her eyes quickly and darting back up.

Dad followed, belatedly as per usual, carrying a black trash bag and a pizza box. "Hey, Caesar, how's it going here? Did you look after everybody?" Dad grinned as he walked past.

Caesar and Empress looked back and forth between the humans, wondering what was going on. Once again, Caesar mused how much simpler it would be if Mom and Dad could speak "dog."

"She smells… sad," Empress whispered as Mom ushered the girl in gushing about how much better she would feel once she got a hot shower and meal and led her upstairs to the guest room. *Her room.*

"She's staying here?" Caesar barked.

"But who is she?" Pharaoh piped.

Caesar didn't know, but he was going to find out. This was his house and family. If this girl was going to live here, the least Mom and Dad could do was tell them. They had some explaining to do.

Does she even have a name? he wondered as he crept up the stairs. Caesar pressed his ear against the bathroom door. He could hear Mom's voice explaining where the towels were, how to turn on the faucet, etc.

The girl only murmured.

The water turned on, and the door handle began to turn.

Caesar ran back to the top of the stairs where he laid down quickly, feigning sleep. Not that Mom would have known he could understand her. For whatever reason, Caesar could understand human talk, but it didn't work the other way. Such a pain.

"Oh, hi, Caesar," Mom said, kneeling down to scratch behind his ears. "What do you think of your new foster sister?"

Foster what? He wondered, opening his eyes and quickly planting kisses all over Mom's hand. *Gosh, he loved her!*

But much sooner than he'd prefer, Mom got up and headed toward the bedroom she shared with Dad. He'd just come up the stairs with a quick ear scratch for Caesar as well.

Taking a chance, Caesar followed them into their bedroom, quickly ducking in before Dad closed the door without a backwards glance.

"So, how's it all going?" Dad asked.

He sounded kind of nervous, Caesar noted. The pomeranian knew his dad was a busy doctor, who worked odd hours and came home smelling of hospitals and sterile cleaning supplies; he wasn't usually nervous.

"She seems… scared, as we expected," Mom responded, continuing, "she's been through so much. Bouncing around foster homes. Living on the streets after her mother's death. And with her father being in jail, well, … it's a lot to take in. I can't imagine what she's going through. I don't know where to start. I wish I would've known about her situation sooner."

Caesar stayed quiet, lying on the edge of the bed on Mom's side. He watched as Dad wrapped Mom in a big hug and kissed her cheek before they both sat at the foot of the bed.

"Well, remember what they said in our classes," Dad reminded her, "we need to make a safe, comfortable environment for her and be available. Trust and connection won't happen overnight. But we can start with a shower, clean clothes, pizza, a bed... and see where it leads us."

"I'd like to see her face," Mom said softly. "Her bangs were hanging so low I haven't even really seen her. I wonder if that's how she feels. I bet it has been a really long time since anyone has seen Destiny. Perhaps ever. Maybe that's where we start?" Mom's voice was brightening. The teacher in her loved kids with her full heart, and she'd always enjoyed a challenge. *You didn't become the first female professor in a male-dominated field at your institution by waiting for people to come to you,* she'd always said. *Sometimes, you just have to go for it.*

Caesar thought on Mom's words. Mom was his hero. And now she was trying to take care of this kid who was clearly struggling. A part of Caesar grew selfish every time she brought someone new home. But then again, that's what he loved about her. She wanted to help everyone she could. And now that meant Destiny. Just as Caesar helped Empress and Pharaoh learn the ropes, he wondered, *maybe there is some way I can help her too?*

Thinking on it, he followed his parents out of the bedroom, but instead of turning toward the stairs as they did, he moved toward the bathroom door and laid down outside it.

Mom turned to him from the top of the stairs and smiled widely, as if she could understand his thoughts. "Good boy, Caesar. I know you'll protect her too."

CHAPTER 5

"Of course, she's nervous. She's talking to a cute boy. He's cute, right?" Empress, now blind, was unable to see the young man talking to Destiny at the party.

Pharaoh cleared his throat noncommittally, while Caesar tried to zero in on their conversation. He didn't like the way the boy was leaning in talking to her in a voice too low for his dog hearing. That seemed shifty.

Destiny appeared nervous, shuffling her feet a little and tracing a scar, that Caesar was now familiar with seeing, which lay hidden under her long-sleeve, black Nirvana shirt. Her choppy hair still hung over her face. One eye peeked through the thick locks.

"I think I should go over there," Caesar declared, glaring toward the boy. "He seems suspicious."

Empress scoffed! "Are you kidding me right now, Caesar? Leave Destiny alone! The last thing she needs is for you to go embarrass her in front of her new crush."

Spluttering, Caesar whipped his head to eye his sibling. "And what is that supposed to mean? Destiny would never be embarrassed by me! Mom told me to protect her."

"Yeah... from like bad guys and stuff, not a cute boy. Now enough of your whining," she said pointedly toward Caesar before turning her head slightly to signal Pharaoh. "Now, tell me everything. Are they holding hands? Is she smiling? Do you think he's the one? Are they gonna kiss?"

"Bleh," Caesar blurted, rolling his eyes. He couldn't listen anymore. As Pharaoh obliged Empress and began to share what was happening in real time, Caesar decided he would get closer. Maybe Empress was right, though. Running up and biting the guy's leg might not be the best way to handle the situation. He could be stealthy. *Maybe I should pee on his shoe instead?*

Skirting the perimeter of the house and lurking in the shadows, Caesar drew closer toward the pair that just happened to be joined by another young man. Caesar remembered hearing he was the older brother to the one Destiny was speaking to. The sons of Dad's boss at the hospital.

Caesar felt his lip baring before he realized he was growling. The boy looked… mean. While the other brother was talking to Destiny, this one seemed to be taunting her. Destiny stopped shuffling and stepped back slightly. She looked… agitated.

"That's it," Caesar growled, running over and barking. *Get away from my girl.*

"Hey, hey. No. Caesar, that's enough," Mom called, leaving her girlfriends momentarily and shooing him away.

He ducked back toward the house, glad to see the boys sauntering off toward the Corn Hole game Dad was playing at. He watched as Mom looked Destiny over and peeked back at him. She put her arm around Destiny and led her into the kitchen.

"Well, you did it. Feel better?"

Caesar glowered at Empress. "You weren't close enough. That other boy was bothering her. I'm gonna go find out what he said."

Empress sniffed but didn't argue with her brother. Everyone knew Caesar had only their best interests in mind. Pharaoh walked, slowly guiding Empress, as Caesar ran ahead to catch the conversation indoors.

"Is everything alright, Destiny?" Mom asked gently as she set a fresh glass of lemonade in front of the girl at the counter.

Caesar wandered in sniffing the floor. He had to keep up his nonchalant act. *Oh score, Cheeto crumbs!*

"I'm fine," Destiny mumbled softly.

"Should I ask everyone to leave? Maybe this has been too much?"

Destiny was shaking her head, but Mom fretted on, more to herself than anyone else. "It's too soon. I should have considered it. I'll have them go. I just wanted our friends to meet you. I'm sorry. It's already been a couple of hours, and besides, the storm clouds are rolling in. No one wants to get caught out in that. I'll take care of it, honey. Don't worry."

With a squeeze of her shoulder, Mom was off to shoo the humans away.

Good riddance, Caesar thought, growing hot again just thinking of that mean human boy. He wished he could ask her what he'd said. But since he couldn't, he settled for a quick lick of her bare ankle to let her know he was there.

"Oh, hi," Destiny replied, wiping her palms on her shorts.

Caesar couldn't be sure, but he liked to think that her monotone voice held a tinge of inflection whenever she was talking to him.

Leaving her lemonade behind, she plopped down on the kitchen floor so she could pet him. He happily obliged, tail wagging and tongue moving so quickly she laughed—actually laughed!—from his rapid kisses.

"Caesar," she griped.

Oops, got her in the nostril, Caesar grinned to himself.

She didn't seem upset, though; she continued to pet him. And for the first time, he got a good glimpse at her face. Her eyes, though surrounded by dark circles and cakey make-up, were big and lively. Dark pools that searched his. Caesar rubbed his face upon her tan cheek. His heart warming to this human, surprising himself.

From what he and his siblings could gather from eavesdropping on Mom and Dad's conversations, Destiny had grown up in Hardin near the Crow Reservation with her mother Shayna. It didn't sound like her father had been around much, and now it seems he'd recently been arrested for drug possession. Caesar didn't understand everything that Mom and Dad talked about, but he could figure out the basics. Mom and Destiny's mom were second-cousins who had grown up together. They had been best friends all through school, played basketball together, danced at Powwows, and gone on to pursue higher educations: the first in their families, which Mom always said with an expression of pride. They'd also fallen for *white guys*, as Mom called them. But where Davina had gone on to pursue Grad School and her PHD, marrying Alex sometime during that period, Destiny's mom had gotten pregnant and moved back in with her parents, never finishing her degree. Mom said the difference was Shayna's boyfriend Scott never respected her or her dreams. And in the end, he left her with a kid and a whole lot of heartache every time he blew back into her life. Shayna had had to try and work to support herself and her daughter and took on caring for her aging parents as well. In a completely and utterly tragic incident, Shayna and her parents had been killed in a car accident on an icy I-90 interstate coming back from a dialysis appointment in Billings last winter.

In that instant, Destiny's mother and grandparents were taken from her. Social Services knew her father was unfit, so they found the closest kin for her to live with: Destiny's uncle. And though they didn't know much about that period, Caesar had a feeling that's when she got that scar. Destiny had been labeled a "delinquent" during that period, frequently running away from her uncle's and couch-surfing. She was known to cut school and smoke cigarettes, though Caesar didn't know what that meant. Her uncle got sick of her, preferring to be on the road a lot, and kicked her out. She then bounced between a few other families before Mom heard about her.

Mom and Shayna had fallen out of touch over the years. Nothing terrible or dramatic, they just went in different directions. Caesar knew Mom beat herself up about it. As soon as she found out that Destiny wasn't doing well and had been booted from her uncle's—who as it turned out was involved in some of the same drug smuggling Scott was—Davina went straight down to the social services office and volunteered to take over Destiny's guardianship. They were cousins—albeit distant—anyhow.

And so, that's how Destiny came here. But it would take a lot of time before she was actually here. Caesar looked into her eyes and found the glazed over expression again. Her time with him had ended, he could tell, and he stepped back to watch her quickly run up the stairs to her room, slamming the door behind her.

Sigh.

CHAPTER 6

"I'm calling a family meeting," Caesar declared one afternoon shortly after the BBQ disaster. Destiny was at her new school and Mom and Dad were at work.

Caesar looked over to see Empress give a very dramatic roll of her head in Pharaoh's general direction. Sometimes he questioned if she really was blind, or if she was just saying it to get more attention. She'd always been one for the dramatics. But at that moment she walked into the table leg as she headed toward his resting spot in the living room. *I take that back*, Caesar grumbled to himself. Walking up and giving Empress a quick sniff and nuzzle to help guide her over.

After a few more moments, Pharaoh ambled over yawning, and Caesar got right to the point.

"Guys, I think we should keep the girl."

Empress burst with squealing laughter. "That's your big declaration? Of course, we're keeping the girl, you bottlehead. Mom brought her here, where else would she go?"

Caesar glowered at her. *Maybe I should have left her stranded amidst the table legs.*

Pharaoh cleared his throat, catching onto Caesar's annoyance. "I think what Empress means, Caesar, is that she has a home here with us... at least for now. You heard Mom and Dad. It isn't final yet. There are 'procedures,' as Mom said, that must be followed."

Caesar harrumphed, his stance wilting slightly. "Oh, I know," he admitted. "I just wanted to make sure we're all in agreement. So, do you want to keep her?"

Empress and Pharaoh paused then. Clearly considering it. And avoiding eye contact with him, which he knew was to be expected from Empress, but Pharaoh too?

"Hey," Caesar perked up, "seriously, guys, do you have a problem with Destiny being here?"

"I—" Pharaoh began, as Empress cut him off.

"She's just... different. And smelly," Empress blurted. "I mean, she's alright. I like when she scratches my tummy. But she's really sad all the time and takes so much of Mom's and Dad's attention away from us."

"You sound a little jealous, Empress."

She sniffed. "Maybe I am," she snapped. "I'm their little girl, not her. All she does is mope around and make Mom and Dad feel bad."

"And the truth comes out," Pharaoh murmured, earning a glare from Empress, though in the completely wrong direction.

"Empress, we don't know what she's been through. Mom and Dad still love us... all of us. But I don't know, I feel like we're supposed to keep her."

Pharaoh's neck outstretched to soak in more of the light coming through the window blinds as he stifled another yawn. "What is it about her that you like, Caesar?"

Caesar paused. *Did he like her?* He honestly wasn't sure what he thought about her. He agreed with Empress. Destiny was a little smelly still. Even after all her baths. It was from her clothes, but she refused to wear anything new that Mom bought her. And she did take a lot of Mom and Dad's attention. She barely talked, and sometimes she seemed closer to a zombie than a living human. And as Pharaoh pointed out, it wasn't certain whether she would stay. But for some reason Caesar felt she was supposed to stay. "I... I think she needs us," he concluded lamely.

"Well, she's here now, but when have Mom and Dad ever asked us what we thought?" Empress pointed out.

And as if on cue, Mom came home early through the door holding a leash. And that leash was attached to something big.

"Oh, for the love," Caesar griped as Mom walked in announcing she'd brought them a "new friend."

CHAPTER 7

"That's it. I'm moving!" Empress announced, marching off, narrowly avoiding the wall as she made her way to her bed. Well, Caesar's bed, actually.

Pharaoh followed her to his enclosure and closed his eyes.

So it was that Caesar stood alone to greet the newest member of the family.

"Guys! Oh, don't be like that. He has nowhere else to go... for now. The shelter called and he needs a safe family to foster him until an adoptive family can be found." Caesar cocked his head at Mom.

"Foster?" he barked, realizing that this meant the dog wasn't here forever. *Good*, he thought, sniffing.

And Empress thinks Destiny stinks.

"Caesar, meet Chief. Be nice," Mom added, unclipping the leash from the dog's collar.

Caesar eyed the dog. Chief was ten times the size of him. No, more like fifty! Chief ran up to him to investigate. A growl escaped before Caesar could help it. Chief bared his very white, very large teeth in response.

"You gotta problem?" he challenged, his dark coat bristling.

Caesar jumped back, glaring yet knowing he'd be no match for the larger dog.

"Hey," Mom snapped in the most authoritative voice Caesar had ever heard her use. Startled, Chief looked back at her.

"Now you listen to me, Chief, you are in my home. So, whatever got you by up until now is going to need to change. In this house, we are respectful and kind. We do not pick fights. And *that*, is my baby. So, you better be nice, or this will be a very quick stop for you," she said in a serious tone as she squatted down to meet his eyes, "do you understand me?"

Caesar burst with affection for his Mom who had stood up for him. *I love you, Mom, thank you!* He piped, tail wagging excitedly.

Chief backed up and sat, his ears down. "Sorry,"

he softly whined.

Mom held his eye a moment longer before reaching out slowly to pet him. "Good boy," she said warmly then. "We'll teach you how to live in a family, okay? You're not on your own anymore. You're safe."

Caesar watched this curiously. Mom spoke as if she thought he could understand. She didn't know that he actually could. Caesar had a million questions for her. Like why on earth she kept bringing pets and kids home, for starters?

He flinched as he felt something brush his shoulder and looked over to find Empress and Pharaoh. They'd heard the growl and had come to their brother. He smiled at them gratefully.

"Let's try again," Mom said with her no-nonsense teacher voice, looking pointedly at Chief. "Guys, this is Chief. Chief, this is Caesar, Empress, and Pharaoh. They are my babies. You will be kind to them, and in return," she paused eyeing the three, "they'll welcome you to our home and show you around, okay?"

Chief looked from her to them and back. She must've taken his calm stance for agreement because she stood up brushing her pantlegs. "Good," she said stepping back a bit to give them a chance to sniff each other in greeting.

Awkwardly, a moment passed before Caesar sighed and stepped forward, "Hello."

Chief stepped closer to take in his scent; Mom leaned in ready to intercede if needed. Caesar held his breath, eyeing the massive jaws.

"Hi," Chief responded. His nose twitching as he took in all the smells and gave a giant lick across Caesar's snout.

"Bleh," Caesar groaned. Sniffing, he then realized, *Wait, that's puppy breath!*

"You're just a pup?"

"Yeah," Chief said, flopping down in front of them, as if tired out from this interaction.

Empress and Pharaoh leaned in to sniff him once he was settled. "Hi," they murmured.

He looked at them with droopy eyes, trembling slightly.

"You're nervous," Caesar observed aloud before catching himself.

Chief squirmed backwards. He quivered and let out a whine. It had been total bravado. *What had this puppy gone through to make him think he needed to fight any dog he came across?*

"Shhh, no, no, it's okay," Empress said, surprising Caesar... and Mom, who had been inches away from petting Chief. Yet as Empress moved forward, Mom's hand froze and then returned to her lap.

Empress stepped forward, unable to see their newest addition, but certainly able to sense the giant puppy. "You don't need to be nervous. You need to be nice, like Mom said, because you're much bigger than us. But not nervous." She nuzzled adding, "You must miss your family. It's scary at first, I know. We'll take care of you, okay?"

Chief cracked an eyelid, his trembling beginning to lessen.

And just like that, Empress walked up and plopped down next to him. Pharaoh followed and settled in next to her. Caesar glanced at Mom, whose eyes looked a little shiny. He walked over and gave her ankle a good lick or two in reassurance. He too settled in next to the sleepy giant.

Chief didn't speak again, giving in to sleep.

Hours later, Mom left to pick up Destiny from school. But before she left, she put together a large kennel in their living room. She had placed a water bowl, dog bed, blanket, and chew toy in there and then led Chief into it. Apparently, she didn't completely trust him to be left alone in the house. Caesar appreciated her concern but had a feeling the puppy would do alright. "Mom's the boss," he explained to Chief. "She'll be back soon though, you heard her?"

Though Chief whined softly the entire time Mom was gone, Caesar, Empress, and Pharaoh all managed a long nap, which was good, because things were about to get complicated.

CHAPTER 8

It all started the day Chief arrived. Up until then, Destiny had been sad, but quietly adjusting to life with them.

But once she came home to the giant puppy, it was as if she was an entirely different person. She was loud. Angry. Yelled and said mean things. She was explosive!

Caesar couldn't understand it, and neither could Mom or Dad.

"What? You think this Rez dog is like me? Is that it? You think I'm some dumb native orphan that needs you to rescue me too? Well, I'm not… and I don't. I hate you," she screamed at Mom before slamming her bedroom door.

Caesar hear her stifled sobs every time she slammed the door.

He didn't get it. *Why didn't she cry in front of Mom and let her help?* Every time Caesar or his siblings were sad, Mom always made it better. He didn't understand any of it.

And as for Chief, the poor pup was terribly confused and felt guilty for being there.

He was a big, lumbering oaf, yes... but he was just a kid. Caesar had learned from his frequent listening ins on Mom and Dad's conversations that Chief had been found in the wild near the Crow Reservation and some Native American battlefield. He and his litter mates had been left orphaned when their mother had died; her body and the abandoned litter found by a rancher. Only two other pups had survived with Chief, and they'd all been quickly brought in and placed in foster homes. Those who found them whispered of their location, as if divine. They'd been discovered next to antlers with one lone eagle feather atop them. It was a sign. A good omen. Mom, being Crow, had picked the male and named him Chief, saying he was already a warrior for having survived for so long in the wild.

It, then, was no wonder he lacked social graces.

He ate messily. He had accidents in the house. He was gassy. He barked too loud. His tail whacked into everyone. And he rolled in everything outside.

As Empress put it, "He's a big dope but he's our big dope." She took it upon herself to be his instructor and was constantly reprimanding his every behavior. He didn't seem to mind, though. If anything, Chief seemed to soak it up. He loved the maternal attention he received from her. Unlike the mean glares—and kicks under the table—he got from Destiny.

Anytime she was in the room, she would radiate anger toward the puppy. Usually, he cowered back or went to his pen when she was in the room. Caesar couldn't figure it out. It was as if he was the source of her troubles. It didn't make sense at all. Chief had never done anything to her.

Caesar tried to talk to her, but it made no difference. Things would be so much easier if she could speak "dog," he thought for the millionth time as he barked and wagged and licked and whined, telling her to go easy on Chief, who had left the room while they had dinner. Destiny bent down and scratched his ears, but her facial expression hadn't changed. She'd started wearing her bangs in front of her eyes again, with that thick, cakey eye makeup.

"I don't know what we're doing wrong, Alex," Davina wept one night while Alex sat beside her and lightly petted Caesar, who pretended to doze on their bed.

"Well, it certainly seems to have gotten worse since you brought Chief home."

Mom pulled away, aghast, "Are you saying this is my fault? Should I take him back? Where would he go?"

Dad shook his head and said in a reassuringly and mild-mannered voice, "No. Your desire to help and your fierce passion is what I love most about you." He kissed her forehead, pulling her into a side embrace. "I just think perhaps we should consider finding a more permanent home for Chief, and slow down on the new additions for a while. You know what they said in our classes, Destiny needs consistency and routine. She's had nothing but scares and changes these past couple years. Her whole life really."

Mom sniffled, sighing. "I suppose you're right. Chief is a handful anyways. Maybe we'd all be better off without him."

Caesar couldn't feign the act anymore. "Wait. You're giving up on him? Just like that," he barked.

Without a word, Dad picked him up and carried

him out of their bedroom. He plopped Caesar in the hall and closed the door in his face.

That had never happened. Caesar was always allowed in their room, and he usually spoke his mind, whether they understood him or not. *What was happening to Mom and Dad?*

"Caesar, what is it? You smell… morose. Is that the right word?" Empress asked, looking toward Pharaoh, he murmured in agreement.

"Shhhh," Caesar whispered hushing her and eyeing the kennel where Chief was once again banished. "Let's go talk outside."

Once through the doggie door, unable to contain his unease, Caesar turned toward his siblings. "Guys, Mom and Dad are going to get rid of Chief. They think he's too much for Destiny. I tried to argue with them, but Dad kicked me out."

"What?" Empress said, her voice pitched high with worry. "They can't get rid of him. I mean I know he's an idiot. And stinks so bad but," she ended plaintively, "but he's ours. He's *my* puppy."

At the same time, Pharaoh added, "They kicked you out?"

Both were very unlike their parents, which worried them.

"Maybe it's Destiny who should go?" Empress grumbled, laying down to gnaw at her right paw as she often did when nervous.

"No," Caesar responded. "Destiny is hurting. She needs us. But what she needs to realize is that Chief needs us too. Why can't she see that?"

"Because she's selfish. And smelly. Have you noticed she's gotten smellier? I can't be the only one," Empress griped.

Pharaoh reached out his neck to peek around the corner.

"What is it, Pharaoh?" Caesar asked, coming to look. Rain droplets splattered the yard. Caesar sighed. Another thunderstorm headed their way. *Great, just great. As if we didn't have enough problems.*

"I thought I heard footsteps." Pharaoh said, interrupting Caesar's thoughts.

Wait, Caesar thought. *Had he?* He and Empress had been talking so much that he may have subconsciously ignored gravel being crushed underfoot.

Empress walked out from the covered patio, raindrops smacking her wiggling nose. "I smell... Cheetos?" She came back under the cover. "Hmm, that's strange."

Just then a spectacular lightning bolt crackled across the sky, followed by a loud boom. "We better get inside," Caesar urged as the rain began to pour.

Mom and Dad had come out from their room and were looking over the house to make sure everyone was alright. Mom stood outside Destiny's door calling to her, but the door was locked.

"She's not answering," Mom said worriedly, coming downstairs.

"Oh, give her some space. She's probably asleep. Thunderstorms aren't anything big to us, Montanans," he smiled, playfully puffing out his chest.

"Oh, please," Mom said swatting at him, but her voice held its usual warmth once more. "You're more scared of thunder than any other man I know," and just as he made to deny it, another boom sounded, and he flinched visibly.

"See!" she laughed, hugging her smaller frame around his. "There, there, I'll protect you," she teased.

Caesar was being hammered with too many thoughts and sounds. He was happy to see his parents acting more like themselves. But Chief was awake and whining. Mom went to him and let him out of his kennel. "It's alright, buddy, it's just a storm. I bet you've been through a lot worse than this huh?"

He leaned into her legs, his giant tail smacking as he happily licked her hands. Mom laughed, and then, as if in realization of her talk with Dad, wiped her palm down her pants and moved away from him.

Caesar's anxiety returned. They really were going to get rid of him. He sighed, before moving to comfort Chief.

"Did I do something wrong?" Chief asked, and then more to himself added, "I'm always messing up."

"No, you're alright, it's just the storm. Mom and Dad are a little anxious about it. Last year lightning started a fire in a field not too far from us. It burned through some of the canyon before the humans could put it out."

Chief's ears perked up nervously.

Caesar internally kicked himself. "Oh, don't worry, there won't be a fire this storm. It's raining already, so we're safe. We just gotta wait it out."

"I don't like storms," Chief said.

"Me either," Caesar said.

"Neither do we," Empress added. She then made her way to comfort the worried Chief. "It's okay though, we'll wait it out together," and then, trying to lift the mood, she quipped, "dog pile!" And flopped on the ground dramatically.

Chief, with a puppy' exuberance, did a little hop before he too circled and plopped on the floor next to Empress.

"Hey," Pharaoh piped in.

"Tortoises too!" Empress amended.

Caesar smiled at them, moving closer to snuggle in as well. He didn't fall asleep like his siblings did, though. He watched as Mom and Dad set out candles and flashlights just in case the power went out. Dad, as he usually did, sat in his favorite chair and turned on the TV, cranking the volume to drown out the storm. Mom shooshed him, motioning him to turn down the volume so as not to wake Destiny. Dad then pointed to the window as another loud boom sounded.

Mom gave in, and they lounged for another hour or two before finally nodding off. Caesar went up to Mom and nuzzled her hand after an hour or so. She sat up drowsily, petting his head before dragging Dad out of his chair. They made their way up to bed.

Caesar remained where he was, recalling his earlier rejection. But his protectiveness was just too strong. He liked knowing everyone was safely in bed before he allowed his eyes to close. With heavy lids, he softly followed his family upstairs to listen at their door and ensure they were going to sleep. He heard their fan switch on, which aided their sleep whether it was one-hundred-degrees or below zero. Dad said he liked the noise. Caesar didn't understand humans, but was comforted when he heard it switch on and the bed creak as they got in.

He then remembered Destiny. He stood at her door, listening. He couldn't hear anything, which was unusual. She wasn't a sound sleeper, and he typically heard her tossing and turning for a good hour or two before falling asleep.

He got down low, which was easy as a small pomeranian, and tried to peer under her door. He couldn't see anything because something was blocking his view. He became alarmed and stared harder. Sniffing and snorting as he searched under the door, his nose perked in recognition. Understanding and worry crept in. An empty Cheeto's bag lay discarded in front of the door with a few loose crumbs on the carpet. No sound was coming from the room. It didn't seem like she was even in there.

And then it hit him! *Cheetos! The footsteps.* He dashed downstairs to tell the others. Destiny must've snuck out her window!

CHAPTER 9

Destiny

The Canyon Creek Battlefield Monument was the only place nearby Destiny could think to escape the rain. Davina had given her a history lecture about the brave Chief Joseph as they passed it once on the drive home.

She ran down Buffalo Trail toward the overhang, the only dry place around here, besides back at Alex and Davina's. But she refused to go back there.

"They're jerks," she mumbled, though shivering through her soaked Rolling Stones long sleeved shirt and ripped jeans, she knew that wasn't true. They had been nothing but kind to her. Things had been getting better even. And then they brought that stupid dog home, and it reminded her of everything back home. She had seen dogs like that. She'd had a few. Mutts. Mongrels is what her dad had called them. Worthless. Unlovable. Just like she felt.

She'd let her guard down, getting caught up in the comfortable ease at the house. Pampered just like Caesar, Empress, and Pharaoh. And then Chief had shown up. Awkward. Ugly. Dirty. And out of place. Just like her. She didn't want the reminder that she didn't belong there. She was just a foster too. Not one of them. Temporary. Forgettable. Not really part of their family.

She needed to get out of there. So, she had run. She hadn't planned to. But the storm had started, and it seemed like a great cover for her to get out unheard. Now, she realized it was idiotic as the rain had turned to hail, and she was pummeled from every side by the dime-size ice.

"Crap," she groaned, shivering and standing under the tiny area. She needed to get away. Her thoughts were scattered but all she could think of was escape. She had learned about Canada in her Seventh Grade Geography class. Just north of Montana. Seemed like a good place to start over. She had no phone. Money. Or passport. She was just a twelve-year-old nobody with a soaked outfit and an attitude.

Stubbornly, she wiped the plastered hair from her face and set her shoulders. Anything was better than living in that house with that dog.

***

While the human girl squatted down to wait out the storm, she missed the pair of golden eyes watching her in the darkness. Wicked laughter lost in the storm.

Razor had been waiting for a child like her to stumble across his area... and he wasn't going to miss this opportunity. He swooped down from sky, screeching his signal. Then twelve pairs of eyes encircled the monument. The human had no idea what trap she had just walked into!

CHAPTER 10

"You really think this is a good idea?" Pharaoh questioned, lumbering behind.

Caesar sighed, "Yes, I do. We all agreed. If we don't go after her, who will?"

"Yes but…. This rain is making it really hard to follow you guys. What if I get lost? I can't smell you in this?"

Caesar stopped, eyeing Empress. The spoiled pom was sopping wet and hovering close to Pharaoh. Looking around, Caesar spied a piece of twine left discarded from someone's bundle of hay. Thinking fast, he picked it up with his teeth, pulling it over.

With Pharaoh's assistance, they were able to make a loop for his neck and one for Empress.

Now tethered together, Empress laughed a little shakily, "I never dreamed I'd be leashed to a turtle."

Pharaoh cleared his throat.

"Tortoise, I mean," she joked.

Caesar smiled, knowing that he'd been able to help and that she was trying to muster some of her old self. And then, "back to the trail," Caesar reminded himself, looking for the muddy footprints they'd followed from their house.

Being in the country, much of the terrain was undisturbed, making fresh footsteps easy to find. On the other hand, it was dark, and the landscape was also forbidding with jutting rocks, overgrown yucca, cactus, and sage plants, and sloping hills and valleys. Her human legs could carry her farther than their tiny legs, and he worried she'd get too far ahead of them. Maybe they'd never find her.

Squinting in the rain, trying—and failing—to come across a Cheeto scent, something shook the bushes behind them. Something big was headed their way.

Empress squeaked, "what was that?"

Caesar panicked, shushing her and trying to think fast. Pharaoh and Empress were no match for whatever it was. And him? Caesar was four pounds of fluff... on a good day. *What had he been thinking bringing them out here?* They'd barely spent any time outdoors in their short lives.

Davina had always cautioned them about rattle snakes, bears, mountain lions, bobcats, coyotes, and wolves. Not to mention big birds like hawks and eagles. There were predators lurking everywhere, and he'd led his siblings right into their midst.

Another stomp and shake.

Caesar looked at his siblings, jumping to stand in front to face the threat, though he knew there was nothing he could do. Then something jumped out from the darkness.

Caesar braced himself, knowing he'd be swallowed up in one bite.

"Hey—did you just lick me?" Caesar cracked an eyelid to see none other than Chief happily circling them, sniffing, licking, and laughing.

"There you are. Where are you guys going?"

"Chief?" Empress was the first to speak, stepping tentatively forward to sniff him.

He gave her a huge lick in response. "Yep, it's me. Where are you going?"

"How did you get out here?" Caesar asked instead. He specifically remembered sneaking out while Chief was still locked in his pen, and Mom and Dad were asleep.

"I woke up, and no one was there," Chief said with a slight quiver to his voice. "You left me?"

"Oh, Chief," Empress murmured, leaning into him. "We didn't want to bring you into this. It could be dangerous."

Caesar peered at him, "But how did you get out?"

Chief, as he often did, flopped down with a heavy sigh, his puppy-ness becoming apparent. "I got scared and… kinda woke up Mom and Dad," he said this last part as if he knew what Caesar's reaction would be before he finished.

"You what? So, they know we're gone? Do they know about Destiny?"

Chief looked at the group. "What happened to Destiny?"

Caesar huffed, and Empress tssked at him.

Before they got into a word war, Pharaoh responded, "Destiny ran away. We realized it during the storm and decided to go after her. We had hoped to bring her home before Mom and Dad even realized we were gone."

"Oh, sorry," Chief said with a sheepish expression. "Well, they know now."

"Yeah, that's pretty obvious. What'd they do?"

Caesar questioned.

"Mom came down first and let me out of my kennel, thinking I needed to go outside. And I did. I ran outside, smelled for you all, and jumped the fence."

"You what?" Caesar said, this time surprised.

Chief lowered his head a little at this. "Mom wasn't very happy with me. She shouted for me to come back and then screamed for Alex to get outside."

And then as an afterthought, he added, "how did you guys get out?"

"We pushed the gate open. Dad never remembers to latch it all the way. Pharaoh leaned with his hard shell against it until it swung open. We closed it behind us."

"Oh," was all Chief said. It seemed they were already losing his attention. The giant puppy's nose was twitching as he sniffed loudly and examined their surroundings.

"Well," Caesar said, surveying the group. "We can either go back to Mom and Dad now that they know we're gone, or keep going and bring Destiny home?"

"Let's find her," Chief said loudly over Empress's hesitant "ummm."

"What?" All three replied, staring at Chief in

shock.

"But she's so mean to you? Why would you?" Empress implored.

Chief dipped his head, not making eye contact, his large puppy body quivering. Caesar didn't think he would respond but was dumbfounded when a moment later, Chief looked up and said, "She is part of our tribe."

And for the first time since Caesar had met Chief, he saw that this wasn't some silly puppy. This was a dog who had known hardship, who had lived on the edge his entire existence, and still believed in a tribe. A family. A pack.

Caesar felt his resolve strengthen and raised his head proudly, though his only came to Chief's ankles, but still. "You're right, Chief, she is one of us."

As Empress added, "and so are you," Chief licked her again affectionately, and she gave a soft laugh before telling him that was enough.

Caesar smiled at his siblings. "Well, let's track down our human," he said resolutely.

CHAPTER 11

The rain was coming down hard now. *Pelting*, as Dad called it. Caesar's heart just panged thinking of his parents and how worried they must be. He had to find Destiny and get everyone home soon… before anyone got hurt. The hill they'd been climbing suddenly began to slope downwards. They'd made it to the valley. Buffalo Trail Road ran through it, and Caesar knew, if Destiny had planned this, a car may have been waiting for her. *We need to get to the road.*

The rain was coming down hard now. Pelting, as Dad called it. Caesar's heart just panged thinking of his parents and how worried they must be. He had to find Destiny and get everyone home soon... before anyone got hurt. The hill they'd been climbing suddenly began to slope downwards. They'd made it to the valley. Buffalo Trail Road ran through it, and Caesar knew, if Destiny had planned this, a car may have been waiting for her. We need to get to the road.

As they made their harried descent, Empress's tether to the ambling tortoise kept her in line, and with Chief's presence helping guide her, they slowly neared the road.

Sniffing, Caesar glanced up. A growl forming in the back of his throat as he searched for the danger.

"Caesar," Empress whispered, "what is it?"

"Do you guys hear that?"

Pharaoh and Chief cocked their heads but after a moment shook them. They didn't hear anything. Caesar walked in a circle, listening.

"Hoo." Empress said.

"I don't know, that's why I was asking you guys. I thought I heard something," Caesar replied tersely.

"No, hoo," Empress replied.

Losing his patience, Caesar rolled his eyes. "No sarcasm, Empress. This is serious." But then he paused as his sister's tiny noise continued to wiggle.

And then he heard it. Not "who" but "hoo." It was the hooting of an owl. And it was close.

Caesar shivered involuntarily. He hated owls. Creepy with their rotating heads and too big for their face eyes. Plus, Mom had always warned them to stay together at night if they went potty, so that they weren't scooped up by an owl. Caesar had always thought it was a thing Mom told them so they'd stay in bed. A children's story. But now, out in the wild at night, he wasn't so sure.

Out of nowhere Chief jumped, bumping Caesar off his feet. "Aahhh," Caesar yelped. Trying to save face, he glowered at the giant puppy, "Hey, watch out!"

"There... It's her!"

Caesar swung his head around to peer in the distance in the direction Chief was facing. Being much taller, Chief was able to see above the tall grasses and scattered rocks. But now with a little focus, Caesar could see what Chief was staring at.

Destiny... and an owl.

It was dragging her—its talons dug into her shoulders, clutching the fabric of her wet shirt— toward a shimmering area off the road. Coyotes, which made Caesar's stomach drop, followed as if in league with the bird. Caesar recognized the location. Though he didn't leave often, he did remember seeing it in passing whenever Mom took him to the vet or groomers.

It was a monument of stone with a small overhang to protect visitors from the elements.

"We have to get down there," Caesar snapped. Though it was dark, he couldn't miss the twisted anguish in Destiny's expression. The owl was hurting her. She was crying out in pain and fear.

Her screams mixed with the screeching owl and howling coyotes.

Chief jumped into action and charged down the hillside recklessly.

"Chief, get back here!" Empress cried, then griped, "Darn his fast legs," trying to keep up, while Pharaoh narrated what was happening for her as they went as quickly as their tiny legs would allow. Caesar was torn between protecting Empress and Pharaoh and rushing off ahead with Chief to get to Destiny. He settled for somewhere in the middle, keeping a pace just behind Chief.

"Watch out," Caesar yelled as he reached the pavement and watched Destiny and the owl, disappear into the shimmering darkness.

Chief had eyes only for Destiny, missing the other shapes forming around them. Luckily, the coyotes seemed intent on following after the owl and disappeared before noticing Chief or the others. The giant pup kept his fast pace and closed the distance, pulling up short near the monument. Caesar followed on his heels, to make sure there was no other threat there, and ordered him to stay seated while Caesar went back for the others.

"I mean it, Chief. Do not go near that area until I get back. Stay."

Chief grumbled, "Who made you Alpha?" under his breath.

Caesar stared at him expressionless, "Mom did."

"Okay, okay. I'll wait here."

"You better," Caesar said before running back down the road to meet up with Empress and Pharaoh.

"Pharaoh said they 'disappeared'... can you please tell this tortoise that I'm in no mood for games. Where is she?" Empress snapped, rainwater spluttering from her snout.

"He's telling the truth," Caesar said, unsteadily, "Though I have no idea how. Come on, I left Chief there and I don't completely trust that he'll still be there when we get back."

"Oh, that puppy knows better. What was he thinking dashing off like that? I am going to have a few words for him, mmmmhmmm." And just like that, Empress had a little more pep in her step as she made her way toward her giant "little" brother.

Caesar led them back, trying to piece together what he'd just seen. An owl… and a coyote gang herding a human girl through a… he couldn't think of the word for it.

And as if reading his mind, Pharaoh said, "portal. A magical portal to another place. It's the only logical answer."

Caesar shot back a glance at him. "Logical?"

"Well, before I came to live with you, I lived with a college student named Tim. He used to listen to a lot of fantasy audiobooks, and places like Narnia and Middle Earth filled our days."

Though still walking hurriedly to get back to Chief, Caesar paused momentarily to look at Pharaoh. "Wait… you had a…"

"Another family?" Empress piped in. "Before us? That means, wait— How old are you?"

Pharaoh chuckled. "I'm fifteen."

"Fifteen?" Caesar and Empress both said together.

And then Caesar added, "What? Why didn't you tell us?"

While Empress added, "What happened to Tim? Did he give you away?"

Pharaoh swallowed, and Caesar looked down. He knew what the response would be.

"You never asked," Pharaoh said quietly, his words just barely audible above the rain droplets hitting the road. "And I..., well, it was easier to put it behind me. Too painful to discuss."

"Because he gave you away?"

"What? NO!" Pharaoh said so forcefully that Empress jumped, though the tether wouldn't allow them to totally separate. He tilted his head up, still walking with them, but clearly in another place entirely.

"Tim's parents got me for him as a present when he was growing up. It was a little touch and go for a while, but they got into a rhythm, and Tim took care of me. He didn't have many friends in school, so he told me all his secrets. What he learned. What he dreamed of. I was his companion. And so, when he graduated high school in Arizona, he decided to move to Montana and attend the college here...."

"Where he met Mom," Caesar supplied the pieces as they moved from the road to the gravel that led to an enclosure where Chief sat obediently.

"Yes, where he met Mom. She was his favorite teacher. He talked about her lectures all the time.

But then one day he couldn't get up. He was tired. And then the next day. And the next."

Upon seeing them, Chief trotted over and gave Empress a soft lick. Together, they sought shelter under an overhang, but all the while, their focus remained on Pharaoh.

"It was cancer. In his bones. My Tim died three months and eleven days later. I didn't know it until after, but he had asked Mom—your Mom—to adopt me since Tim's parents hadn't ever really been animal people. And he worried they'd give me away. And so, Mom came to the apartment—Tim was in Graduate School by that time and didn't live on campus anymore—after his funeral and packed me up. And brought me home to you guys. I'd never met another animal before."

Exhale. Caesar felt like he'd been punched in the gut. Years. For years he had lived with Pharaoh and had not ever thought to ask him of his life prior to their house. He had just assumed he'd come from a litter—or whatever the turtle equivalent is called—like he and Empress had.

"That's why you're so big," Empress said softly. You were already grown and had lived a life without us. "I'm so sorry, Pharaoh. We're the worst! We thought you were a baby, but it's so obvious now.

You were so smart. Oh, Pharaoh, I'm so sorry!" Empress said sniffling.

"You are not the worst. You two—and you—," he paused to look at Chief, "are my family. I was alone a lot when Tim was at school or work. Now, I'm never alone. I'm glad of the company."

"I'm glad we know of Tim now, Pharaoh. I'm sorry it took us so long," Caesar said, meaning it.

Pharaoh nodded just once, his eyes glassy, but then seemed to shake it off, peering at the shimmering area. "The portal," he started again. "It must be a portal, like from the stories Tim used to read with me."

Caesar's attention snapped back to the stone monument that shimmered like it was alive with light. "Well, I guess that means we have to go through it too... if we still want to reach Destiny?" His anger began to rise again picturing the terror on her face. He stepped toward it and then looked back.

"Wait," Chief said, hopping back over. "Let me go first, just in case."

Caesar was about to argue, but Chief gave him no choice, he turned back and said, "She doesn't like me, so if this doesn't work out, at least you're still safe. And you never know, there could be a bear or something waiting on the other side?"

Caesar's eyes widened.

"Bear?" Empress squeaked.

Without another word, the large puppy jumped toward the shimmering stone and… he too disappeared.

Caesar's heart thundered in his chest. He waited two heartbeats, and without hearing any screams on the other side, jumped as well.

Empress and Pharaoh, quick on his heels, followed right behind him into the unknown.

CHAPTER 12

"It looks familiar," Chief mumbled once they were together on the other side.

Trying to see through the falling rain, Caesar blinked rapidly. He was right. They stood still in the valley surveying what they could in the conditions. "It looks the same."

"But it smells... different," Empress said, nose wiggling upwards as she sniffed their surroundings. "It's cleaner."

"Of course, it is," Caesar began to say, thinking it the rain, but then paused.

"There are no human things here," Pharaoh observed, his neck outstretched.

And that's when Caesar understood. They had passed through the shimmering monument and wound up in the exact same spot, but without the stone… or a road for that matter. The rain was beginning to lessen, and where once had been Buffalo Trail now stood swaying grasses, wild yucca, cacti, sage, and stones.

"Where did it all go?" Caesar asked.

Pharaoh met his eyes, "I think we've passed into a parallel dimension. The same place and most likely time, but without human civilization."

Before they could inquire further, a shrill scream from far beyond their location broke their concentration.

"Destiny," Caesar breathed.

"There is one human still here," Chief said, a growl in his throat. "And the coyotes are hurting her!"

The giant puppy leapt into action and began tracking their trail.

Empress tugged on her tether, "Come on, Pharaoh. Don't lose my puppy!"

Caesar's pulse quickened as he too followed Chief, yelling for him to slow down. He had felt guilty earlier when they were trying to find Destiny the runaway. Now he wondered if he'd ever be able to get them all home. *Will we ever see Mom and Dad again?* he wondered. His heart panged with worry, but he knew Destiny needed to be their focus. Find the girl, somehow avoid being eaten by coyotes—he shivered at the thought—and after that, he'd find a way to get them all home. He had to.

"Over here," Chief called. He had stopped his drive forward and was circling an area.

"Cheeto crumbs!" Empress crooned.

As Caesar approached and sniffed, he too smelled Cheeto debris on the ground. She must have sat here pressing her gooey fingers in the dirt, at least momentarily. Besides the Cheeto smell was a strand of her dark hair. They couldn't be far. "We're on the right track! Good work, Chief. Let's go!"

Picking back up on the trail, the group carried on. Chief in the lead followed by Caesar with Pharaoh and Empress tottering behind. Yet as they were moving through the valley toward a few trees, the bushes began to shake. Caesar collided with Chief as they skittered to a halt.

"Hey, watch it!" Empress snapped as she walked into the boys' tumble.

"Shh," Pharaoh warned them, peering in the darkness.

The bush shook again, and this time Empress squeaked, "what is it?"

Chief jumped up and stood in front of the tiny animals. Caesar wanted to urge him to move behind since he was younger, but didn't have the breath for it, for just then something in the darkness growled.

"I don't want any trouble, just keep moving and no one will get hurt," a low voice murmured.

"A bear," Empress whispered, fear leaking into her voice.

"Yes," the voice said. "Ha! Yes, yeah, that's right... I'm a bear. You better run before I come out. I can see you trembling. Wait until you can see me. You will rue your slow departure then. Hurry. Run, you little animals."

Empress scrunched up her face, sniffing the air. "Wait, hold on a minute. I know that smell... it's a... it's a... bunny?"

"Is not. No. I'm a bear," the voice warbled. "You will tremble. Rue the day and fear me and—"

"What's happening to your voice? You don't sound as tough now?" Caesar paused, listening. "I think Empress is right. Why would a bear still be hiding?"

"I'm not hiding, I'm... ummmm.... thinking. Plotting."

"We don't mean you any harm, Mr. Bunny," Pharaoh said in a kindly voice.

Caesar quickly agreed. "Yeah. We're looking for our sister—a human. Have you seen her?"

"Hypothetically, if it was to turn out that I'm a bunny and not a bear, would you promise not to hurt me?"

Empress sighed exasperated, "Dear, look at us, besides our big puppy, do we look like we even could?"

The bush was silent for a moment, and then it shook as a small black and white bunny hopped into view.

"Whoa," Caesar said, leaning forward, "you don't look like the bunnies near our house."

"What's he look like? Describe!" Empress whispered tersely to Pharaoh, hating to miss any detail.

The bunny, no longer feigning the menacing voice, spoke with a higher pitch, "Oh, I know. I'm domesticated. Or rather, was domesticated. My family dumped me by the monument years back and I've been here ever since."

"Oh, that's terrible," Empress said quickly. "What's your name?"

The bunny hopped closer. "They called me Barney. Barney the Bunny. Real original huh?"

Pharaoh gave a soft chuckle, but Caesar, hearing the hurt in the bunny's voice, winced.

"But I prefer to be called Bilbo," and then as if an aside, the bunny whispered, "it's way cooler."

Empress snorted, "That doesn't sound any better than Barney, if you ask me."

Caesar could have kicked her. "Empress," he hissed, looking at the bunny's crestfallen expression.

Pharaoh spluttered, "Ah, I'm sorry for my companion, she isn't familiar with the famous Hobbit and his journey. That is a great literary name. Valiant even."

The bunny puffed up a little under Pharaoh's praise.

"Alright then, Bilbo, it is," Caesar said, hurriedly adding, "have you seen our human?"

The bunny's ears quivered as he nodded hurriedly. "They passed by this way… that's why I was so threatening earlier. I thought you were with them."

Empress snuffled at the mention of "threatening," and this time Caesar was close enough to bump her. "Well, can you tell us what you saw? Which way they went?"

"It's not good. Razor doesn't usually come this close to the edge."

"Edge? Razor? What do you mean?" Caesar pressed.

"Razor is bad. A real bad bird," Bilbo started.

Caesar remembered the owl. He shivered involuntarily.

Bilbo continued, "He's been getting a gang together for a couple years. Their territory is to the east but occasionally, he'll fly out here alone. Like he's scouting for something. I heard from the prairie dogs nearby that he'd passed through a little north of here last week. He killed one of them on his way. He must've gathered those coyotes from the other side—the edge. You're in the animal zone now. No humans here."

Caesar felt like his head was spinning. "How does it work? Can we get back to the human side?"

Bilbo snickered, "Yeah, look for the glowing air shaped like the monument stone you came through, due west… though I don't know why you'd want to go back. If you ask me, you're better off here. Humans are nothing but trouble."

"Not all humans are bad," Pharaoh said kindly, "we live with some wonderful ones."

"You're pets?" Bilbo said as if just realizing it.

"Umm… duh," Empress snapped, "do I look like I've been living in the wild all my life?"

Caesar couldn't help but laugh. Turning to look at his sister, who was sopping wet from the storm with muddy paws and a few twigs caught in her tail, he thought her in worse condition than the bunny.

"Hey, stop that. What's so funny?" Empress implored, growing crankier by the moment.

Chief erupted in chuckles, falling on his back, legs kicking the air playfully. Even a few measured chuckles came from Pharaoh, though he'd tried to tuck his head near his shell to keep her from hearing. It only made the sound reverberate more. Bilbo just sat there taking it all in.

"Bilbo?" a voice piped, startling them all.

"It's alright, Mona, they don't mean us any harm… well, most of them, that is," Bilbo said, eyeing Empress, but since she was blind, she missed the snub.

Just then a small field mouse scurried up a stone nearby Bilbo, where they conferred quietly. "Do you promise not to hurt my friend here too?"

"Of course," Caesar said, sobering, "we just want to find Destiny, our human, and get home so Mom and Dad can stop worrying. Can you help us? You said the owl—Razor—his territory is east? Is that where they're headed?"

The mouse whispered more to Bilbo, and then he turned to address the others. "Mona, sent her spies after them and has some reconnaissance for us... so long as you promise not to hurt us, or expose her operation here."

"Spies?" Pharaoh asked, surprised.

"Wow... I mean, yes. We won't hurt anyone here, right guys?" Caesar said loudly, ensuring that his siblings knew this wasn't time for any silliness. Empress and Chief both nodded solemnly and Pharaoh ahemmed.

Mona the mouse seemed appeased by this. "Okay, team, here's what we know," she began in a squeaky yet authoritative voice. "At twenty-one hundred hours, a pack of twelve coyotes passed through the edge with a human in tow, led by the infamous outlaw, Razor. We've been after this guy for a while, but having the advantage of flight, he continually escapes capture. Now, by my estimates they're making for the Rims and beyond toward Bison country. There is no good reason to bring a human here unless—"

"Unless?" Caesar asked nervously.

The mouse, though teeny, seemed to loom ominously upon the rock as she looked them over. "Unless he means to take her to the bones."

"What bones?" Empress squeaked, adding, "And where did you learn to talk like that?"

"It's like something from an action movie," Pharaoh whispered.

"Yeah, like the movies Dad watches!" Chief agreed.

The mouse rolled her eyes, "It's like this... My old owner used to run intel for the government. The Pentagon actually. Military guy. Super secretive stuff. But then he died a year ago, and his kids brought me to Montana, and then decided they didn't want me anymore."

Caesar began to apologize, but she held up a tiny paw to cut him off. "No time, do you want the girl back? If so, we have to move."

"Wait, you're coming with us?" Caesar asked.

"Of course, I'm coming with you... and so is my entire troop. We've been waiting for a moment to catch Razor in the act. This is it. We have a multitude of witnesses that saw him break the animal zone code by bringing a human here. I have enough evidence to throw the book at him, figuratively speaking."

Caesar gaped. He had thought he was tough... until he met Mona the military mouse.

"Alright, what are you waiting for? It's time to move out." Upon her word, skittering steps sounded all around them. There were mice everywhere!

"Thank you, Bilbo," Pharaoh began, thinking the bunny would stay behind.

"What? You didn't think I was gonna stay behind while you all head out on this adventure, did you?"

CHAPTER 13

As the contingent of mice headed out, Caesar and his siblings followed, somewhat bewildered. Soon, animals from all over the prairie and forested areas joined their party. Word must have spread, and within the hour, they were greeted by prairie dogs, raccoons, robins, crows, a few red-winged blackbirds, and even a sheep! It seemed to have wandered through the edge. Though after trying to strike a conversation with it, Caesar decided it was a pretty slow-witted sheep. It didn't even seem to mind being separated from its flock. He munched and chewed and mozied along.

As their party plodded, Caesar fretted. He knew

despite being on the move that he and his party could not move at the speed of coyotes and owls. He worried they'd be too late. He needed to ask more about the bones, or whatever else Mona had alluded to, but his eyes were getting droopy and his brain foggy. They had left in the evening, and it was nearing midnight before Mona called for them to halt and rest.

"You guys, okay?" Caesar asked his siblings gathering around. A few "yeahs" or "mmhmmms" was all he received.

Chief plopped on the sodden ground, and Empress and Pharaoh snuggled in beside him. Though Caesar wanted nothing more than to lie down beside his siblings, he worried they were too exposed.

A tiny paw patted his foot. He looked down to find Mona. "Don't worry, kid, I'll take first watch. My team and I will stagger watches until sunup. We have a long march tomorrow, so get some rest. Your group look like you could use it... being pampered pets and all." With another pat and a twitch of her whiskers, she saluted, then turned on her heel, barking out orders in her squeaky yet authoritative voice.

Caesar bristled at Mona's final words. *We're not*

pampered... we're— he cut off. Looking at Empress and Pharaoh. The mouse was right. Chief was holding up rather well, though he was a puppy and loved his rest, he had spent months in the wild. He could handle this, whereas Caesar, Empress, and Pharaoh had always been indoor pets. "Dang, we are pampered," Caesar grumbled to himself, "what was I thinking?" He bemoaned silently as he laid down next to Empress who was shivering slightly in her sleep.

She murmured, "I miss my bed."

Pampered indeed, he thought.

"Psst..."

Caesar blinked. *What was that?*

"Psst... shh, wake up," a voice squawked in the dark.

Caesar sat up more alert; Empress snored lightly beside him. Chief shifted slightly, and Caesar thought he was going to get up. Good. Maybe having the giant puppy awake would help calm Caesar's nerves. He didn't see anyone.

A sound erupted in the night air. *Gross!* Caesar held his breath. While asleep, Chief managed to shift enough to let out a giant fart. And now Empress was awake.

"Ewww, Chief, what have we talked about?" She said snippily rolling on her other side.

Coughing, Caesar stepped forward.

"That was disgusting," a voice murmured.

Caesar yelped to see a black and white bird sitting not far from them atop a stone. "Magpie," he growled, recognizing the wily bird. "What do you want?"

"My, my. Not a morning dog, I take it?"

A growl came from behind Caesar, and he and the magpie jumped to see a pair of eyes watching them. "Are you okay, Caesar?"

"Chief!" Caesar squeaked. "Yes, good… you're up." He continued in a stronger voice, "What do you want, Magpie?"

"I bring word of the human. There is another way to get to her. I know a shortcut. You can head them off and leave these meddling vermin to their own deceptions. Mona doesn't care about the girl, only bringing down Razor."

Empress snorted, joining the conversation. "And why would we listen to you? Everyone knows magpies aren't to be trusted. You chatter and grouse and live off roadkill. That's disgusting," she emphasized.

Caesar couldn't deny her. Empress had basically

summed up his thoughts of magpies entirely. "They're no better than crows," Mom had always said. "The only thing worse are grackles!"

The magpie stared at them levelly. "Contrary to what you might think, I do care. Very much."

"Why? You don't know us or her. What's in it for you?" Caesar couldn't hide his frustration. He really wasn't a 'morning dog.'

"Well, to stop Razor from using the bones, of course. I don't want to be stuck in the animal zone, I like, as you said, 'roadkill.' Without roads, it gets a whole lot harder for me to find meals." He said the last part slow and deliberate. Clearly, trying to antagonize Empress, who let out an uncharacteristic little growl.

"You're a vile—" Empress began, but Pharaoh, who had slowly ambled over, cut in.

"Did you say 'stuck in the animal zone?' What are these bones?"

"Awww," the magpie jumped slightly, anticipation leaking into his words, "you really don't know? Ha! That is so like Mona to not share all the details. What the mouse conveniently forgot to mention were the bones... and the legend surrounding it."

Chief's tummy rumbled, and he looked at them in exasperation.

"Hold on, Chief," Empress ordered. "We need to hear this... whether or not we'll believe it."

The puppy flopped down, and the magpie continued. "Legend has it there is a place, east of here, where a mighty bison laid under a lone pine tree upon the prairie and died of old age. His body wasted away to eventually leave only his bones."

"Yes, sadly that happens," Pharaoh began.

"Yet, it is not only bison bones though. Then there's the buck, which became lost in a storm and had to take refuge near the bones, only to fall ill and die atop the bones, eventually leaving only his bones and a large pair of antlers behind. That does not happen every day." He paused for effect. And what never happens are bison and buck bones mixed with eagle bones and feathers. That never happens.... Except one time. It is a sacred place. In this land, where the bison roam and the eagles soar, to find their bones entangled is an omen. Razor—and many living on this side of the barrier—believe that, should a native child of this land touch and lay the bones to rest, it will seal the animal zone and keep humans from ever marring this sacred land again." The magpie concluded.

Caesar felt his heartrate rising. "But what about Destiny? What happens to her if she does this?"

"They'll kill her, of course," the bird said ominously.

"Kill?" Empress squeaked, while Chief growled.

"Well, that is why we're going after them with Mona," Pharaoh responded.

Caesar nodded, "Right. We're going to make sure that doesn't happen."

"Ahh, as you say," the magpie replied coolly, "and yet, why do you so easily put your trust in the mouse?"

"She wants to take down Razor, she has an army of mice ready to help," Caesar said. "She and Bilbo want to help us save, Destiny."

"Oh my, is that what you heard... or what you wanted to hear?" The magpie said softly. "As I recall, she said she would help bring down Razor. Your girl wasn't mentioned. You see, she's tricked you. While she does want your assistance fighting off Razor and his coyotes, she's taking the long route, for she knows that if she can stall a bit longer the barrier will be sealed, and then Razor can be dealt with."

"Ha!" Empress snorted, "So typical of a magpie to tell crazy lies. Come on, Caesar, our puppy needs food... and so do I," she added, a tiny growl of her stomach escaping.

Pharoah paused, "Hang on, I would like to hear

more, if it's alright with you?"

Empress stopped, "Pharaoh? You can't be serious. He's totally lying!"

Caesar looked from Pharaoh back to the bird. He didn't like the magpie, but he did trust Pharaoh's intuition. "Alright, anything else you haven't shared?"

The magpie cackled. "Oh, yes, but if you think back, you already know that what I'm saying is true. Mona and Bilbo... do you recall how they came here? Discarded pets. Mona despises humans; there is a deep hatred burning in her toward them, and so, while she is angry about Razor bringing a human into the animal zone, she isn't beyond letting him seal us here before 'throwing the book at him' as she says. She wants to bring down Razor while also making it impossible for you or her to leave. No more humans ever."

Caesar gasped. *It couldn't be? Could it?* He thought back through yesterday's conversations with Mona and Bilbo. They both had expressed hurt and dislike for their past owners. Caesar felt himself growing more and more unsure.

"I won't lie or mislead you. My intentions are this: I like going between the human and animal zones. It keeps me fed. And I have friends on both sides. So, we have a mutual interest to ensure that girl never makes it to the bones. If you're able to save her, it must be before she lifts them. Otherwise, Razor— and Mona for that matter—will no longer have a use for her... alive."

Caesar looked at his siblings feeling unsure.

"But if you don't believe me still. Go have a listen. She's sitting up talking about this very thing with Bilbo. I overheard much of their conversation this night," the magpie whispered, and flapped a wing in the direction of a tiny light.

The siblings peered in unison, Empress turning the wrong way, of course. There was a small light. Caesar tilted his head listening. He needed to get closer.

"I'm gonna go check it out," he told his siblings.

"I'll go with you," Chief said jumping up.

"No," Caesar shushed him. "I'm smaller and can blend into the dark with my black coat. They won't even know I'm there."

Chief looked uncertain, glancing between him and Empress.

Empress gave a slight nod. Even without her sight, she still often could sense the pup's body language. *Maternal instinct*, she called it.

"Be careful," Pharaoh said.

Caesar gulped but held his head high. "I will."

On soft feet, Caesar padded through the darkness toward the sliver of light. *What was causing it?* he wondered.

Stealthily, he kept quiet—mostly—besides almost walking directly into a cactus. He narrowly missed it, froze, then listened. Nothing.

Creeping again he arrived outside the circle of light where voices could be heard.

Next to a miniscule fire, in a circle of small stones, sat Mona and Bilbo, their heads pressed together in hushed conversation.

"Yes, but I still think you're being too hasty. I like them. Give them a chance." Caesar recognized Bilbo's voice.

"Ha! A chance? Those pampered pets wouldn't last two days on their own here. They're soft, Bilbo. Too acclimated to human comforts. We need the big one though. He looks strong. So, we'll wait to get rid of them until after the battle. He could probably take down three or more coyotes with a swipe of his paw. I've been waiting for someone like him to appear for a long time. We have to take this chance. Besides, once those stupid puff balls—and the giant lizard— find their girl dead, it'll be easy work to be done with them too."

"I don't know, Mona. It's risky. What if the big one

turns on us after losing his siblings?"

"Nah, Bilbo, you sound like a nag. As soon as the job's done, the animal zone will be rid of the killer in the sky and his coyote gang. Then, I'll emerge—uncontested—as leader of the prairie. My rodent express reports there are no predators around. All the wolves, bears, mountain lions, bobcats are still in the mountains. None have been spotted this season. We will eliminate the major birds and coyotes on the plains. And then, we'll never have to fear again. Well, except for, an occasional badger or fox... but we can deal with them. Once we have that giant dog on our side, we'll be invulnerable!"

Caesar couldn't believe what he was hearing! The magpie was telling the truth. And it was worse than he'd expected. Mona meant to kill them! She wanted to be ruler of this place.

He eyed her perched on a small stone. She was tiny... smaller than him, and that was saying something. She said she hated the human world and yet sat eating a cube of cheese with a box of matches nearby.

She must have her "rodent express" gather supplies from the other side. *What would she do once that wasn't an option anymore?*

Caesar couldn't think about that right now. He

had to get back to his siblings. He had to—

"Sir," a squeaky, yet crisp voice cut into Caesar's panic.

"What is it?" Mona asked, sternly, eyeing another mouse that had crept up beside her.

"First rays of light have been spotted on the eastern horizon. Should we break camp?"

Mona surveyed the land in the direction the mouse was pointing. Mona laughed coolly. "What's the hurry? Let's let those pampered pets sleep another few hours. We don't want to be too hasty," she laughed darkly.

The mouse smiled smugly before saluting and running off.

Caesar fled. He had to gather his siblings immediately.

"The magpie is telling the truth. Mona plans to kill us and keep Chief as her bodyguard. We need to get out of here. NOW! But quietly," he told them in an urgent whisper, arriving moments later. "Let's go!"

"Follow me," the magpie said, lifting silently into the air to guide them. "I know another way."

CHAPTER 14

"Are you guys sure about this? I can't see anything," Empress whined.

Caesar knew Empress was cranky when she began stating the obvious. Of course, she couldn't see anything. Besides, none of them could. It was dark upon the sloped rimrocks that jutted from the earth, creating a natural barrier enclosing the valley. Not far from here, in the human zone, Mom and Dad were probably driving around looking for them.

Caesar wanted to go to them but shook himself. He needed to focus. Stick to the plan. And make sure no one heard Empress's whining from down below.

He turned around to peer at his sister, still

tethered to Pharaoh, who trudged slowly up the slope.

Chief ran circles around them, his energy seeming boundless.

"Can you shut her up?" the magpie croaked, landing near Caesar on a small pine sapling. "Sounds echo up here, I told you that. We must keep quiet."

They had scurried off as soon as Caesar returned with word of Mona's betrayal. The magpie, that called himself Enzo after the restaurant roof he'd been born on, had spoken of a faster yet harder route, one that the mice couldn't handle. The slopes of the rims were dotted with cacti, yucca, sage, clusters of trees, and clumps of bushes. There were also boulders to go around and smaller stones and loose gravel to walk over. And beyond that—and the elevation—was the ever-present threat of predators. While Mona had believed most of them were near the mountains, Enzo had insisted they stay quiet and aware for every once in a while, a stray coyote, mountain lion, fox, or wolverine would appear... not to mention rattle snakes.

Empress cried out, having bumped into a cactus. "I can't do this!"

"Shhhh, shhhh, Empress," Caesar said imploringly.

"Be quiet. Here, let me help you."

Pharaoh had stopped and was looking from her to Caesar worriedly.

Chief joined them, stopping his scouting loops. "Are you okay, Empress?" he asked, nuzzling her tear-strewn cheek.

Empress looked in rough shape, hair going every which way, and bits of dirt and plant matted in her fur. Her ears and tail were down, and Caesar knew from her body language alone that she was scared.

But what could he do? He was only four pounds himself. He could walk on her other side, but she'd still most likely bump into stuff. It was too dark for Caesar and Pharaoh to see everything.

"I will walk closer to you, Empress," he began, and then paused, eyeing Chief.

The puppy was huge… they could make that work to their advantage, couldn't they?

"I have an idea," Caesar said quickly, calling Enzo to assist him with his plan.

Moments later, despite Empress's doubts, they had secured her onto Chief's back. Enzo, having grabbed the tether from Pharaoh and Empress in his talons, flew it around so that it looped from Chief's neck to Empress's small body. None of them having opposable thumbs to tie it improvised by stabbing cactus thorns, securing the ends to the rest of the cord. With a tug it would most likely come apart, but it was something, at least for now. Empress was ordered to stay still, and so long as Chief walked levelly, it would hopefully get them through until daylight.

Caesar was once more impressed by the puppy. Yes, he did lap around, bump into things, and have terrible gas, but he was so good and gentle with Empress. Caesar exhaled, knowing Empress was okay for now, and they could step up the pace. Well, most of them. Pharaoh still ambled behind but he seemed more confident now that his shift as Empress's guide was over.

"We're not far from the top. Let's go!" Enzo cawed, as he lifted above their heads to lead the way.

As dawn began to break, the pet party and one bossy magpie crested the hill.

"Wow," Pharaoh breathed as a brilliant sunrise greeted them. No cars, airplanes, smoke, or power lines to diminish the gorgeous view. Vivid pink, magenta, violet, and golden rays flooded the night sky upon the horizon.

"Wow is right," Caesar said. "The Big Sky State,"

he recalled Mom calling it.

Chief trotted up, pausing, his nose in the air. "This is familiar."

Caesar looked at the giant puppy. "It's still not too far from our home, on the other side."

"No, it reminds me of…," he trailed off, suddenly shy.

"What is it, Chief?" Empress cooed from atop his back.

It still never ceased to amaze Caesar how sweet Empress was toward Chief.

"It reminds me of my other family. My litter. We lived out—in this. The wild. That way," he gestured eastward with his nose.

"That's the direction we're heading," Enzo cawed, cutting in. "We must hurry. Mona will know that you've left now that the sun is up."

Caesar looked back down the sloped rimrocks and rolling hillside. "You don't think they'll follow, do you?"

Enzo cocked his head, then shook it. "I don't think so… but that doesn't mean they won't try to cut us off. We need to get ahead of them. Come on."

And with that, he lifted into the air, once again leading the way.

Caesar and his siblings followed, thankful for the

oncoming warmth of the sun. "It's gonna be okay, guys," the tiny black pomeranian said reassuringly, mostly for himself.

The morning was uneventful, minus the one-time Chief jumped over a large cactus rather than going around it, and Empress nearly fell off. She had quite a few words for the puppy, and Caesar and Pharaoh shared a pitying look as her tirade went on... forever.

Just as they were cresting another hillside heading toward the Yellowstone River, according to Enzo, a sharp voice chilled them all.

"Stop right there or I'll shoot."

Chief barked, the back of his neck bristling.

The magpie cawed anxiously, swooping upwards into the sky.

Caesar yelled for everyone to calm down.

"I'm warning you," the voice hollered from behind a cluster of ponderosa pine trees.

Chief stepped forward, growling.

"That's it. Fire!"

Caesar didn't have time to think, he just yelled "DOWN." And dived for the ground, while Pharaoh spun so any ammo would ricochet from his shell. Enzo swept into the air. That left Chief—and Empress who was still tied to his back—exposed.

"Aaaah," Chief yelped while Empress shrieked, "WHAT IS THAT SMELL?"

Caesar's eyes watered with the acrid odor. His eyes were blurry, but he could just make out Chief hopping around with Empress flopping on his back, wailing.

He ran to them. "Are you guys, okay?" He skidded to a halt. "Bleh," he gagged.

"Skunk," Enzo said dryly. "Really? Was that necessary?" The magpie directed his gaze to the trees.

A pair of noses popped out from the lowest branches. It was hard to see clearly standing this close to Chief, who had taken most of the spray. Empress flopped like a dying fish out of water atop his back... ever the dramatic.

"GET ME DOWN! I'm dying. I'll kill him. I'll kill whoever just did that. Do you hear me? This smell is NEVER getting out of my fur. Waaaaaaahhhhhh," Empress cried out belligerently.

Caesar looked toward Pharaoh and Enzo. "Let's get her down." As he did so, he called out, "Whoever you are, we don't want any more trouble. We're just trying to find our lost human. We think she was taken this way."

"A human?" a voice asked tentatively.

Caesar spun. "Yes, have you seen her?"

"No," the voice answered quickly. Too quickly.

"Are you sure?" Caesar pressed.

The branches shook and whispers emerged as the pair spoke. They were arguing but Caesar could only hear a word or two.

Enzo cawed. "Will you come out already? We won't hurt you."

"What about that one?" a voice asked, hesitantly.

Caesar knew it meant Empress. "She's all bark but no bite. Trust me," he said.

Empress growled, "Wanna bet?"

"She's blind, and now with this overpowering scent everywhere it's removed any ounce of her ability to sniff you out. Trust me, you're safe."

"For now," Empress said in a clipped voice, for just then, two tiny faces emerged from the trees. A black and white, silky skunk... and a... black, prickly porcupine!

"Porcupine?" Pharaoh breathed. "Thank goodness, you didn't shoot!"

"Did that boulder just talk?" The skunk whispered loudly to his companion.

The porcupine tittered nervously but answered Pharaoh. "Uhh, yeah, I was the second shot. If it was needed. Usually, Sam's shot does the trick."

"Sam?" Caesar asked looking toward the skunk. "That's you, I take it?"

"Yeah," the skunk replied, shyly.

They're just kids, Caesar realized, taking in their size and hesitance now that they were out in the open. "We don't mean you any harm. We really are looking for a human. Our sister was taken by Razor the owl. Have you seen them?"

The porcupine looked at Sam the skunk. "Well—" he began, then paused when Sam shook his head.

Pharaoh stepped closer. The two had obviously never seen a Sulcata Tortoise before. Caesar recognized their childlike curiosity.

"You can tell us. And then we'll leave you alone if that's what you want. We really need to find her before Razor or his coyotes hurt her. Can you help us please? If you know something, it's best to tell the truth." Pharaoh said solemnly.

"Oh, alright, but promise you won't hurt us?" Sam pressed, stepping closer. The porcupine close on his heels.

"I promise," Pharaoh said, and Caesar agreed.

Meanwhile, Chief, now freed from the burden of carrying Empress, was rolling in the dirt to help get rid of the smell.

"I'm Pete," the porcupine introduced. "The

coyotes passed through here last night... surrounding a human. I've never seen a human before, but we hid and saw very little from our hiding spot. Coyotes are bad news."

"Was she okay?" Caesar asked quickly.

The two looked at each other again. "She... is alive," Sam said.

Caesar felt his stomach drop. "Was she hurt? How long ago did you see her? Which way?"

"Slow down, Caesar," Enzo cawed. "Let them tell us and then we will head off."

"She was crying, maybe a little hurt," Pete the porcupine said, "and the owl warned her if she didn't go faster, he'd let the coyotes eat her. He flew behind her pushing her with his talons."

Empress gasped, momentarily forgetting her disheveled state.

"But I can't be sure, like I said, we were hiding," Pete said.

Enzo soothed, "Razor can't kill her, at least until after they get to the bones. There's still time. But we need to get to the river."

"Bones?" Sam peeped.

Hurriedly, Caesar filled them in on what he knew, Mona's betrayal, and made their formal introductions. The pair had never crossed over to the human zone. They had found each other and become best friends after both losing their families to a hard winter.

"She's an orphan?" Sam asked.

"Like us?" Pete replied.

"She was," Caesar corrected. "But we're her family now, and we've come to rescue her."

The pair pressed their heads together, and then turned back as if they'd just decided something.

"We're coming with you," Pete declared while Sam nodded.

Caesar was surprised, "Umm," he began, not knowing how to let them down nicely.

"We could use their firing skills," the bird mused.

Caesar glanced at Enzo. He reasoned allies would be a help if they were to fight off a band of coyotes. But they're just kids.

"It's dangerous," Caesar warned.

"We've lived here our whole lives," Sam said assuredly, "we know how to survive out here. She doesn't. You'll need our help."

Caesar wanted to say they'd probably only been alive for a matter of months, but Pharaoh cut him off.

"If you feel obliged to help, we will gladly welcome you to the cause."

The porcupine and skunk looked wide-eyed at the tortoise and nodded reverently. The wise tortoise had that effect on people.

"Well, I suppose we should get going then," Caesar said.

"Wait a minute," Empress snapped. "If they're coming, then they have to do something first."

The two looked nervously at each other and back to the angered pomeranian.

"You owe me and my puppy an apology. We're gonna stink for weeks!"

Caesar laughed and nodded at the two who apologized for firing upon Chief and Empress.

"Why did you 'fire'? Have you had to do that before?" Pharaoh asked.

Pete scowled, "Yes… from the raiders. Can't be too careful."

"Raiders?" Caesar said nervously, looking around.

"They only come at night," Sam said, trying to reassure them. "He's talking about the raccoons. Nasty fellows. They always try to steal our food. So, we've taken to firing upon them. We," he cut off, suddenly looking embarrassed.

"What?" Caesar asked, genuinely curious.

"Well, I thought you were one of them at first. You and her at least. You're kinda small and well…"

"YOU THOUGHT I WAS A RACCOON?!" Empress shrieked, seeming to take more offense to this than being sprayed by the skunk.

Enzo squawked, flapping oddly as he collapsed on a jutting stone. Caesar worried only for a moment before realizing the bird was laughing. This lifted Caesar's spirit, and soon he and all the animals were laughing.

"You guys, knock it off!" Empress yelled, stamping her dirty—and very smelly—tiny paw.

Finally, after their laughing subsided, stinky Empress was resecured atop a stinky Chief, and the party took off toward their Destiny.

CHAPTER 15

Chief's tummy rumbled loudly—again. Caesar felt his own squirming from hunger. The sun's rays were beating down, and the tiny dog began feeling more and more lightheaded.

"Enzo," Caesar called toward the bird overhead. "We need food and water." Glancing over his siblings and their new friends, he could tell they all needed a break.

"Food?" the magpie questioned.

Caesar scowled, "Ummm yeah…. We've been walking all day and haven't eaten. Aren't you hungry?"

"Me? Oh no, I dined on the tastiest deer carcass

yesterday afternoon on Molt Road."

"Bleh," Empress snapped in disgust.

"Well," the bird paused, "what do you eat?"

"Dog food and treats," Empress whined. "I doubt that there's any here! No magical dog food tree."

"Magic tree?" Pete piped up.

"Yeah, the tree. We'll take you there. It's close!" Sam exclaimed.

"She was being sarcastic, guys. There's no such thing as a magic tree," Caesar said, growing more impatient with each tummy rumble.

"Awwwww," Enzo murmured. "Yes, the tree. Alright, I'll adjust our bearings. This way."

Caesar blinked. "Hold on."

But Enzo swept forward in the air, and Pete and Sam quickened their pace... *so this wasn't a joke?* Caesar couldn't be sure.

Pharaoh nodded his head and began following, as did Chief and Empress, who didn't have a choice since she was strapped to Chief's back.

Caesar stood there a moment longer. *What the heck are they doing?*

"It better be a Cheeto tree! Oooh, or better yet, Doritos!" Empress called after them.

Chief agreed, quickening his pace.

Caesar didn't know what to expect, but he

followed, and soon was surprised when they crested the next hill to find a large apple tree.

"Apples?" Pharaoh said aloud. "Those aren't native to Montana, are they?"

"Nope," Enzo agreed. "There are a few random trees throughout the prairie. Every once in a while an animal who crosses over will bring seeds back with them—either in possession or through digestion."

"Wait a minute," Empress snapped. "Are you saying that some animal pooped out an apple seed and that's where this tree came from?"

"Pretty much," Sam said, laughing. "Isn't it great?"

Apparently poop jokes were a big hit on this side too, Caesar laughed.

Chuckling, the siblings—well, all besides Empress who grumbled the entire time—walked excitedly to the tree. Soon her hunger won out though, and thanks to Enzo's flying and dive-bomb maneuvers, enough apples littered the ground.

Dogs don't usually eat whole apples, but Caesar knew in this case it would be alright, as long as they didn't eat the seeds, he cautioned his siblings. It was either that—or grass, he reasoned, looking over at Pharaoh who was happily munching on a patch of tall grass and flowering weeds.

Distracted with his meal, Caesar took a moment

to realize that something seemed off. It was suddenly too quiet. He looked around. His siblings were all eating. Sam, Pete, and Enzo were chatting under the tree in the shade. So, what was it that seemed wrong?

Caesar peered upwards, and then it hit him. Moments earlier there had been flocks of birds, gaggles of Canadian geese, and little chirps and tweets coming from the sky and the tree branches. Now, they were gone. All was still.

And that's when he heard rustling followed by a deep growl.

"Guys," Caesar said, alarmed, looking around.

Enzo cried shrilly, "Lion! Watch out!" as he swept upwards, hastily taking flight.

From behind them, a mountain lion emerged. "Mmmmm, I'll eat well tonight," it purred lowly, its yellow eyes flicking around to catch every single one of them in his sights.

"FIRE!" Caesar barked, before jumping toward his siblings and then tearing off down the hillside in the direction Enzo led.

Sam and Pete were already in position, and Caesar narrowly avoided the stink and quill assault. That seemed to take the mountain lion off guard, and Caesar heard him suck in his breath as the potent skunk spray cloud enveloped the lion, his roar following.

Knowing they only had moments and that the tortoise was going too slow, Caesar stayed at Pharaoh's side.

Pete and Sam hurriedly skittered past them with the lion quick on their heels. Quills prickled his face, and his eyes—if possible—emanated an even greater desire to kill.

"Hurry! Leave him, Caesar!" Enzo cawed from the air.

Caesar's heart thundered in his chest, but he would never leave his brother. His tiny paw slid on the loose top layer of dirt, and Caesar got a crazy idea. Looking back, he saw the cat was gaining on them. *It was either crazy or dead*, he reasoned.

"Pharaoh, I need you to stop walking."

"What did he just say!?" Caesar heard Empress's shrill cry ahead of them.

Pharaoh was doing his best to run, but let's just say, no one ever wrote a story about a tortoise outpacing a hare. It was all about strategy, in that old kids' story, wasn't it? And that's what Caesar needed.

"Trust me, Pharaoh. When I say 'now,' lift or tuck your limbs and head as best you can."

His command was punctuated with a growl from

behind.

Caesar yelled, "NOW!"

And, ever the trusting companion, Pharaoh, obediently tucked and ducked. As the large cat pounced, his paws struck Pharaoh's shell, yet with limbs lifted, the momentum sent Pharaoh surfing down the hillside. Caesar leapt at the last second, just out of reach from the swipe of the mountain lion's paw and landed on top of Pharaoh's shell.

Teetering on his tortoise shell surfboard, trying to keep his balance, Caesar snuck a glance. Because the hillside was so steep, Pharaoh gained incredible speed and soon passed Sam and Pete and Chief nearly before coming to the bottom—mostly unscathed. A few bumps and bruises from the sparse plants and rocks, but that was better than being turtle soup!

"Hurry! River is just there!" Enzo called from above.

The mountain cat charged and roared savagely.

Maybe not turtle soup, but pomeranian wasn't off the menu just yet, Caesar considered as he tried to urge Pharaoh to his feet and continue their "run."

They drew near the Yellowstone River, and soon the ground changed from dry dirt, gravel, and prickly plants to spongey silt. Caesar's paws grew sticky and weighted down in the wet soil.

"Oh no," he said aloud, as the cat, much more adept to running on this substance, swept in from the side and skidded to a stop right in front of them, cutting off their route with his back to the river.

"Ha! You stupid domesticated animals never do learn, do you? There is a food chain in the natural world... and you're," he paused licking his lips, "the food." The mountain lion purred as he paced in front of them, ensuring none of the party escaped to the river.

Empress whined, involuntarily, and the cat seized upon it.

"End the game now, and I'll make sure you don't feel... much," the cat growled, saliva dripping from his wicked grin.

All of a sudden, Chief—who had shaken off Empress—leapt from the side, and all one-hundred-pounds of the former Rez dog slammed into the unsuspecting mountain lion.

From his vantage point overhead, Enzo squawked, "RUN! Get to River!"

Pharaoh, Sam, and Pete moved immediately, helping usher Empress along, despite her cries to save Chief... and for the porcupine not to poke her or else.

Caesar was torn. He looked back to see the mountain lion punch with his two forepaws while standing on his back legs wrestling Chief. Chief soared a few feet from the impact. Caesar felt helpless. He was only four-pounds! *What could he possibly do to help?* He looked around panicked while trying to ignore Enzo's caws of alarm.

His eyes fell on a stick. A weathered tree branch that must have come ashore. He ran to it, dipping his head to bite the end and lift it. He tipped on his side, dropping it.

A yelp from behind caused him to glance back and see the mountain lion raking his claws across one of Chief's shoulders. Red blood trailed from the wound.

Caesar frantically dropped his head to the side and chomped on the branch. Chief's posture had changed. He was tired and in pain. The lion was toying with him, but Caesar knew they were down to seconds before the cat lunged and killed him.

And so the tiny pomeranian and his big stick ran into battle to rescue his big, little brother.

Boing. The stick sounded as it collided with the mountain lion's rear end. The cat roared angrily—from surprise more than pain—Caesar knew. He backed up. The seething mountain lion now headed for him, which let Chief off the hook for the time being.

Caesar took a few steps backward, unwilling to take his eyes off the cat. He was small and quick. *Maybe that could work to his advantage?* he wondered to himself.

But before he had to do anything, he heard a caw and a *thwack.*

Enzo flew in, clawing at the mountain lion's eyes, distracting him. And then, the oddest thing happened. Amidst the clawing, Enzo yelled for Caesar to "duck," and then a flying projectile struck the cat mid-chest. And then another. And another. And another! *Thwack thwack thwack.*

Caesar knelt low in the spongey soil but twisted his head to peer toward the river. A creature was manning a wooden device. A—a—beaver? Impossible! Caesar felt he must be dead. The cat really had eaten him.

Suddenly something wet fell on Caesar's head. He looked up to see frothy saliva streaming down one side of Chief's face and dripping onto his.

"Ack," Caesar said, trying to wipe his face on his leg. Standing, he realized the cat was down, but....

"What are you waiting for, you dolts? RUN to River!" Enzo cawed angrily.

Caesar jumped up and was glad to see Chief was

able to run with him. His shoulder looked raw, but it was a surface wound. The bleeding had mostly stopped.

Caesar looked ahead and noticed the beaver frantically waving them over and onto a—ferry! "Come on!" he shouted.

Caesar and Chief dived for the floating vessel, and the beaver immediately pushed off with a wooden pole.

The river drew them inwards to its current and away from the shoreline. They watched as the cat slowly began to roll over and shake itself from head to toe. Its head swung back over to them, considering, as if wondering whether getting wet would be worth it or not. Deciding against the plunge, he limped off and headed back up the hill to terrorize some other unsuspecting animal.

"Phew!" Caesar sighed, collapsing. Through exhausted eyes, he glimpsed Empress attending to Chief's wounds. She licked and nuzzled and lectured and praised.

"Oh, my brave puppy. My poor, wonderful, brave puppy," she cooed over and over.

Chief took it all in stride and nuzzled Empress affectionately. "I'll be alright, don't worry."

"Well, that was a close one," the bird observed

before introducing the group to his long-time friend, River.

River! All that time Enzo had been saying run to River, not to *the* river. "It pays to have friends," Caesar quipped, drowsily.

"You all rest. You look like you could use it. We can visit in a few hours," the beaver told them in a kindly voice.

Caesar cracked an eyelid, observing his siblings already piled up, Sam and Pete nearby, also resting. He looked toward the bird, who cocked his head and then nodded to him. "River knows the way. I will wake you if there is any more trouble. You'll wanna rest before we catch up with the coyotes," Enzo said quietly. "That will be an even bigger fight."

A shiver ran down Caesar's spine. "Hold on, Destiny," he whispered, closing his eyes, before drifting off to sleep.

CHAPTER 16

Destiny

"Oww, stop! You're hurting me!" Destiny cried, twisting her neck around to see ruffled feathers and sharp black talons clawing at her back.

"Oww, you're hurting me," the owl mimicked in an evil voice. "I told you to walk faster. Unless you do so, I'll help you along, human," Razor spat.

Destiny quickened her pace. She couldn't believe any of this was happening. It still seemed like at any moment she'd wake up but judging by the pink pinch marks along her arms, she knew this was happening in real time. The bird pushed off roughly, and she stumbled, just barely catching her balance.

"Watch it," a coyote growled nipping at her leg. Two more appearing as if from thin air.

She screamed but knew she had to keep moving or else Razor would come back. Her shoulders were on fire as if someone held a flame to her skin. His talons had repeatedly dug into her. The bloody marks had dried, her shirt along with them, causing her to stifle and sob each time her tattered shirt tugged too hard on the wounds.

She glanced a look to see Razor sweeping over them into the night sky. His huge wings keeping him aloft, while his yellow, terrible eyes observed everything around him.

It had been a spectacular sunset—one that, had she been home, she would have watched with Davina and Alex... and the pets, no doubt.

Home, she thought. *Was it really her home?* She hadn't thought so but look where running away had gotten her. Now she was, against all odds, a human captive in an animal's world. A place where she could communicate with them and where they ruled. An evil owl and a pack of angry coyotes that had abducted her and led her toward some unknown destination. She trembled just thinking about it.

Please don't let them eat me. She didn't know to whom she prayed, but only looked upwards at the emerging stars as the vibrant sunset colors faded to dusk.

Having lived in Montana her whole life, some of the landmarks looked familiar. It was odd without the presence of humans—no roads, streetlights, power lines, buildings, cars, or planes. But she felt like she recognized this area. *Maybe*, she wondered. *Or, maybe you're hallucinating,* she countered.

They had been walking non-stop, only pausing for minimal breaks, as coyotes rested or hunted. There was no mention of her own physical needs. She thought back. She'd rested her eyes, at least four times. No full sleep, and no food since being here. They'd been on the move for at least twenty-four hours. The owl and coyotes grumbled about not sleeping away the day, as was their habit, but dared not slow their pace. What might be after them Destiny did not know.

She had at the owl's prodding, drank as commanded, as the coyotes did on all fours at a pond, and then once again at the river. But that was it. She had wondered if it was the Yellowstone River but couldn't be sure. For all she knew she was dreaming. Or on another planet. Or dead! Maybe this was what it is like when you die. You're thrown into a nightmare and relive all your greatest mistakes.

"Why did I run away?" she whispered aloud, a tear streaking her face. She knew no one was coming for her. Her parents, or rather, Davina and Alex didn't know where she was. She hadn't said goodbye. Hadn't left a note or anything. They were probably glad to be rid of her anyway. Who wouldn't be? She was a mess. Mean and moody. Taking out all her problems and insecurities on them... and that stupid dog.

She bit her lip, a fragment of her anger returning. It had all started when they brought home Chief. Why did Davina have to do it? It was going great, and then that dog showed up and reminded her of everything. Who she really was... an orphan from the Rez. Dirty. And unwanted. Just like that dog. And so, she'd run... no plan at all. And here she was, paying for her mistake.

The coyotes howled, drawing Destiny from her thoughts. She knew the signal meant she could sit for a few minutes and rest her aching feet. She continued thinking as she did so. Wailing inwardly. The worst part, she realized, was that a small part of her kept thinking that help would come. *Somehow*— she stopped herself. "You're being an idiot," she murmured aloud. "No one is coming." And though she could tell herself that a thousand times, for some reason when she closed her eyes, a tiny black pomeranian filled her dreams. "I wish you were coming, Caesar," she whispered, even though she knew it was impossible.

She glanced up to see the full moon come forward but shuddered as an owl cut through the night air, across the moon's glow. She squeezed her eyes shut, even if for a moment, and pictured herself back home. With Alex, Davina, and the pets. Even the big one. She pictured her bed with the fluffy, new purple comforter and pillows Davina had purchased for her. She smiled thinking of Alex's cheesy jokes and Davina's epic stories. Pet cuddles and unlimited snacks. Destiny tried to will herself back to that time. But it was no use. Before she'd been able to fully fall asleep, there were yips and snarls, and soon coyotes were yapping at her to get moving. Her stomach lurched at the sound. She didn't resist though, but again began her stumbling march across the prairie heading East. For what purpose, she didn't know... but she feared it wouldn't end well.

CHAPTER 17

Caesar sneezed and shook his head, delighted in the best dream: he was jumping on Mom and Dad's bed while they put away laundry. He loved that game. He usually tried to steal a sock or two when Dad wasn't watching. But a buzzing in his ears and nostrils woke him.

"Bleh," he garbled, choking as a swarm of mosquitoes swept all around him. He shook his head vigorously and swatted with his tiny paw. The cloud passed on, and he was able to look around.

He and his companions were still floating on the makeshift ferry, led by a scrappy beaver. It was dark, the moon's giant orb glowing upon the water. Snores and the chirp of crickets echoed softly off the water and canyon.

"How do you feel?" The beaver asked him.

Caesar perked up, having been unable to talk to him earlier after their scary run-in with the mountain lion. It appeared his siblings and their tag-alongs were all still asleep. Enzo sat perched on the pole the beaver had used at the shoreline, his lids closed in sleep.

"I—" Caesar began, then stepped closer, not wanting to wake anyone. "I feel better, thank you," he said softly. And followed up quickly with, "how did you build all of this?" Caesar was awed by the contraptions and innovations.

"Ah," River said shyly, "well, years ago, my sister ran away to the human side. She said she wanted more adventure. My father had died, and my mother was sick with worry. I volunteered to go after her and bring her home."

Caesar couldn't believe it. "But it's a huge world! How did you know where to look? Did you find her?"

The beaver smiled warmly, "That's when I met Enzo. We've been friends ever since. He must've been able to tell that I was lost and offered to travel with me to find her—which we did eventually. In that time, we had holed up at a water conservation area in Billings, close to the zoo. We snuck in one night and I met others of my kind. There, they told me remarkable stories of devices and inventions that they'd seen on the human side. I hung around that area—the conservation and the zoo—for months learning and observing humans and their machines. I've always been curious by nature, and so once, I eventually found my sister—she turned up one day at the conservation area—we came back together, and I started building. I've been trying things ever since."

Caesar was impressed by the story. "Do you make them all up yourself?"

"Ha! Well, some of them, to be sure," the beaver explained, "But mostly, Enzo brings back information and ideas from his observations in the human world, and then I try it." He turned toward the towering device that he'd used to lob rocks at the mountain lion. This one is mine. I based it off a story I heard about a trebuchet that humans used. I think that's how you say it."

"Ah," a voice interrupted. "Yes, trebuchets... you may know it as a catapult, Caesar," Pharaoh said, clambering over to them after freeing himself from Chief's large back leg.

"A catapult," River repeated, testing out the word.

"Yes, they are like trebuchets, but used for smaller objects. You've built a fine one, Mr. Beaver," Pharaoh said, sagely.

Caesar smiled to him, glad to see he'd come out of the hillside surf unhurt.

The beaver's whiskers quivered from the praise, but otherwise made no other indication that he'd heard the tortoise. "Being that I'm a beaver and not a man," River explained. "I have the sling shoot horizontally, as you saw, versus vertically as the humans do. The object thrown won't go as far, but it can go far enough. The precision of one's shot is what really matters. I've had a lot of practice, but even that, well…," River paused. "I got lucky today. I don't usually have such good aim."

"Well, we're glad you did, otherwise…," Caesar gulped, unable to speak aloud what might have been. Instead turning his attention to their river route. "So, are we close?"

"Not quite," Enzo cut in, joining them at the stern. "The river continues further east. Then we'll have to get off. Then, we'll follow the Bighorn River, which flows into the Yellowstone, and then make our way toward the Battlefield."

"Battlefield?" Caesar couldn't hide the squeak in his voice.

"Oh yes, while it is only prairie on this side, I have the layout memorized from the human zone. Many years ago, before Montana became a state, there was a big battle led by the Sioux and Cheyenne Indians against the 7th U.S. Cavalry. This guy named Custer led the charge and died there. It was a huge victory for the Native Americans, and the bones of many U.S. soldiers littered the ground. Some are still buried there."

"More bones," Pharaoh said ominously. "But why are we going there?"

"It is a sacred spot because that's where we'll find the bison, buck, and eagle bones—powerful spirits in the native stories. We'll find Razor and the girl there. He's taking her toward the battlefield... to the bones," Enzo said solemnly.

Caesar's head was swimming with information. Some of what Enzo said reminded the pomeranian of Mom's stories. Davina, being a history professor, told many stories and enjoyed watching historical movies. Caesar thought he remembered hearing her talk about the Battle of the Little Bighorn... it sounded like it might be the same thing, but he couldn't remember all the details. He shook his head. Battles, bones, this was too much for Caesar. He was just a pet!

"Alright then," he said trying to sound more confident than he felt. "When do we get off?"

"Soon," River said. "We're nearing the bend. The current will pick up too much once the Bighorn River flows into this one. Tributaries get tricky. I'll have to let you off," he paused looking at the sky that was becoming a pretty pink and gold with the dawn. "By the time the sun crests the horizon, we need to go ashore."

Caesar nodded, turning to wake his siblings. He had a frightful scare when Pete the Porcupine, sat up, quills going rigid. "Who's there?"

"Don't shoot!" Caesar cried, ducking.

"Pete, would you stop that. They're with us, remember?" Sam said crankily, leaning into a full body stretch.

"Ah, sorry," Pete murmured.

Empress and Chief sat up, yawning and stretching, and still reeking of skunk. "You guys should rinse off," Caesar said.

Empress sniffed, haughtily, but having done so must've given her a good whiff of her scent because she began coughing. "Yuck! Caesar's right. I need a bath. But I can't see anything. Is it safe for me to go swimming?"

"I have a solution for that," River said, his good-natured, even voice interrupting her fretting.

"I'll go first," Chief said, wincing slightly as he took a few steps. The wounds on his shoulder didn't look good, but he dove in and began making slow laps around their ferry.

"My puppy!" Empress cried looking around. "Chief, you big dope! You weren't supposed to go without me. Are you okay out there?"

"I'm fine, Empress. I've swum in rivers lots of times," Chief replied mildly.

River was fiddling with some wooden levers and pulleys, and soon two poles strapped with netting began to move out from the ferry and over the water. The net was shallow and only dipped a foot or so in the water.

"What is that for?" Caesar asked, curiously.

River laughed, sounding slightly embarrassed. "Ah, well, every great inventor has a few not-so-great inventions." He looked at it, and wiped a paw over his brow, continuing, "it was supposed to help me catch debris from the water... especially extra food. Maybe skim some plants, algae, or twigs. So far," he sounded embarrassed now, "it's really only caught a dead fish and a turtle... on accident," he exclaimed, looking at Pharaoh's outraged expression.

"The turtle was fine, don't worry. But I think this should work for you to take a quick dip, Empress. You can sit on the netting—you're light enough—and it will be deep enough for you to be fully submerged, but in a safe, contained way. You're only a foot off the ferry so you won't get lost."

Empress' nose wiggled as she tried to sniff out what River described.

"Come on, Empress," Chief called. "I'll swim near you."

"Oh, you sweet thing, I'm supposed to take care of you, not the other way around," Empress cooed, clearly happy to be tended by the giant puppy.

Caesar rolled his eyes but held his tongue. He was glad that Chief and Empress were keeping an eye on one another, figuratively speaking.

River led Empress to the net, and as she jumped in, spluttered, and griped to Chief for not warning her about the cold water, Caesar let his attention wander.

He wanted desperately to find Destiny, but now that they were getting closer. He needed to plan. What were they going to do when they found her? How were they supposed to fight off coyotes and a crazed owl? And what happens if crazy Mona showed back up?

Enzo hopped onto the pole to study Caesar. "I think we are having similar thoughts," he began after a moment. "It's probably time to start talking tactics."

Pharaoh ambled over, and soon the three were in a discussion over how best to beat coyotes. They needed weapons or muscle. Or both! The definitely needed more animals on their side, they concluded.

"Aaaaahhhhhh!" Empress shrieked.

Caesar's four feet left the ground as he spun in terror, expecting to find his sister dead or injured. But she was fine. Squinting, he walked toward the edge where she was soaking in the shallow netted water.

"Empress, what the heck?"

"Something touched my leg!" she cried, looking around her, unable to identify anything.

Chief growled suddenly, lashing out in the water.

"Pleas-s-s-s-se, pleas-s-s-s-se, I mean you no trouble!" a raspy voice, whined.

"Hold on there, Chief," River called, coming closer. "Ho! Is that you, Buster?"

"Yesssssss," the voice rasped.

And Caesar sucked in his breath as he saw what was speaking—it was a bull snake in the water...

swimming! It cut a path around Chief's splashing body, to pop it's head up near River.

"What brings you this far east?" River asked.

He must know him, Caesar realized, perking up, but before anyone could speak, Empress shrieked. "A snake? That's it! Get me out of here!" She began to flop like a fish in the net.

River sighed. "Hold on, Buster." And he came quickly to his pulleys and was able to bring the net back atop the ferry. As Empress climbed out, the ferry tilted momentarily as Chief climbed up, wincing from his shoulder wound. It looked better having been cleaned from the river water, at least, and the skunk odor wasn't nearly as strong.

As both Chief and Empress shook out and then huddled together, Caesar turned back to the conversation.

The snake Buster was whispering softly to River. Enzo was hopping from one foot to the other, cawing intermittingly.

"What is it? What has he heard?" Caesar asked.

Enzo ceased his hopping but spun around. "Buster overheard a flock of wild turkeys talking about their near run-in with a pack of coyotes to some antelope a day ago. The pack is headed east with a human girl."

Caesar sucked in his breath again, his heart rate soaring. "And?" he pressed.

"And, worse... he also heard from a racoon family further down the Yellowstone, that Mona has been sighted. She's still behind us... but in pursuit. The raccoons said she's warning everyone to look out for a group of dangerous pets from the other side."

"So, we're caught between the coyotes and the mice," Caesar said. And though mice didn't usually scare him, Caesar knew Mona was no average house mouse. She was out for revenge! "We need a strategy if we're ever going to survive this place."

"S-s-s-s-trategy... s-s-s-s-neaking... i-s-s-s-s my s-s-s-s-specialty," the snake rasped. "If I can come aboard, I have a few ideas-s-s-s."

"Absolutely not," Empress's shrill voice exclaimed. "No snakes!"

Caesar growled softly, "Empress, be nice. We need all the help we can get."

"Buster has been my friend for years, Ma'am," River cut in. "He's always welcome aboard my barge." And though he said it kindly, his message was clear. River was the one in charge here... it was his ferry they were on, after all.

Empress, not having a comeback, sniffed, turned, accidentally rammed into Chief's hindleg, and promptly sat down.

As the snake slithered aboard the ferry, Caesar tried to stifle a shiver. Snakes were creepy. Mom had always warned them to stay away from them, but this one seemed nice. Though, he racked his brain trying to remember if Bull Snakes ate meat. *Hopefully not pomeranians!*

CHAPTER 18

Sniff. Sniff. Sniff sniff sniff. SNIFF.

"Chief, what are you doing?" Caesar snapped as his stomach let out another growl.

Sniff. Sniff. Sniff sniff sniff. S-N-I-F-F.

Caesar cocked his head to see the giant puppy's nose in overdrive. Chief was standing up on all fours, seeming to have forgotten about his injured shoulder. His ears were perked up and before Caesar could speak a word, the big dog took off, diving into the river (much shallower in this spot) and quickly clambered ashore.

"MY PUPPY!" Empress shrieked, having awoken to a giant splash. "What is he doing?" Empress demanded to the group.

Caesar looked from her to the puppy on the shore, bewildered. "River, we—"

"I gotcha. I'm pulling ashore now. Just give me a moment," the kindly beaver replied, his brows furrowed.

As soon as the dog had made it ashore, Enzo lifted into the air to follow. He cawed, hovering over some brambles and bushes.

Caesar's heart hammered in his chest.

Chief barked on... but was it with glee or terror?

After another moment, the ferry pulled ashore, and the siblings—plus a skunk and porcupine—carefully piled out onto the beach. River remained at his post but followed them with his eyes.

Caesar hopped over some branches and river rocks to discover what had caught his brother's attention.

"FOOD!" The puppy barked happily.

Pharaoh bumped into Caesar, who had stopped walking abruptly.

"Well," Caesar said, relaxing, "you certainly have a good nose."

Chief's tail wagged rapidly, and soon Empress sniffed him out and began her maternal tirade. Chief, as usual, took it in stride and licked Empress's cheek.

He had found a treasure trove! Wild asparagus stocks stood amidst the marshy brambles, and in a low nest were Canadian goose eggs. "Chief, how did you—" Caesar began.

"I remembered this place. I could smell it. I've been here before. When I was wild." Chief explained, adding, "one egg each." He said, and Caesar was surprised by his mature tone, as he eyed Sam the skunk who was going back for another.

"Well, porcupines don't eat eggs, so I thought…" Sam paused, eyeing Chief, who stepped closer, "I thought… I'll put Pete's back," he concluded lamely. "Yeah, that's all."

Pete jerked his head, as if to silently shut up his friend.

Caesar laughed, coming closer to sniff the weeds and eggs.

"Umm… can someone please tell me what we're eating?"

Pharaoh was near Empress, rolling an egg to her. Caesar knew he wouldn't eat one. And beavers didn't eat eggs. He eyed Enzo, who shook his head and flew toward the ferry.

That left five eggs (including the one Empress had and excluding the one Sam had already eaten). Chief, Sam, Empress, and Caesar.

"Chief should get two since he found them... and since he's bigger," Caesar declared. And then he proceeded to roll an egg over to his spot and... *now what,* he wondered. He looked at Chief, who didn't hold back but grabbed an egg in his large mouth and chomped down, shell and all.

"Guys. Not kidding. I'm not eating this. It smells gross... oh wait," she left off, looking to her side where Sam sat. "It's you."

Some things never change, Caesar sighed. Take, for instance, his sassy sister, who even in a different "zone" and surrounded by new friends still spouted off with her big 'tude.

"Empress," Chief stopped mid-crunch to look at her. "That isn't very polite. You always tell me I need to be nicer."

Sam, whose shoulders had slumped a little as he scooted away from the saucy pomeranian, leaned to whisper to Pete.

Empress, who had pretended not to hear Chief, was rolling the egg around in front of her with one tiny paw.

"Empress," Chief growled, and Empress winced.

"Oh, alright," she spat, "I'm sorry, Sam. I didn't mean anything by it."

"It's okay. I guess I deserved that after spraying

you yesterday," he replied.

"Hmm, yeah... I think you're right," she said, then glancing toward Chief's general location, added, "I forgive you for that, and... you're welcome to sit by me." Considering, she perked up, "and can you show me what I'm supposed to do with this thing?"

Sam licked his lips eyeing the egg, "Yeah, sure—"

Pete poked him with his bristling quills.

"Ouch," Sam said, jumping away from Pete. "Okay, okay, I'm not gonna steal her food. Calm down, Pete."

The porcupine, taking him at his word, mozied off to munch some vegetation, like Pharaoh, preferring it over the eggs.

Caesar, who had successfully cracked his egg and licked the insides clean, turned back to Chief, whose nose was now buried in the asparagus shoots.

"Hey, Chief," Caesar started, "What did you mean that you've been here before? You think it's the same from the other side... even the plants in this area? Do you know where we're headed?"

Chief swallowed, a bit of green hanging out from his lips, saying, "It's familiar. There should be elderberries up that way," he added, sniffing again.

Caesar digested the information, as well as the raw egg. It wasn't too bad. Still, he'd prefer dog food and table scraps over it, but... not bad.

Just as he was going to press Chief for more information, Enzo swept over the brambles, squawking, "RUN!"

Caesar's pulse rocketed. *Is the mountain lion back?* He swiveled his head and saw to his dismay that Empress had run directly into Pete, whose quills had prickled with alarm. She was crying, and Chief and Pharaoh were already trying console her while leading her away. But which way?

Caesar jumped over to his friends, trying to glimpse which direction Enzo had flown. No giant cats had pounced, nor had he heard a growl. *Was this some kind of prank?*

He rushed to Empress's side and gave her a quick lick of reassurance. "Are you okay?"

"Yeah," she whimpered.

Caesar was relieved to see that she wasn't bleeding anywhere. Hopefully it had just been startlement. She'd be alright. Still—he was on edge.

"We need to get out of here. Did you guys see where Enzo went?"

Before anyone could answer him, the bird swept in to clutch at his fur. "Come on, what are you still doing here?"

"But where is it? I haven't seen the mountain lion.

Which way do we go?"

Enzo replied, but his voice was drowned by a loud, incoming hum.

"It's an aerial assault!" Pharaoh dropped his composure and cried with alarm.

Shadows passed overhead, and Caesar looked up just in time to see a gaggle of geese sighting them, beginning their angry descent.

"Run!" He yelled, as geese—upset with their nest being raided—dove in for the attack.

The party took off away from the river and in the direction of some trees where the magpie flew.

A wet, sticky substance hit Caesar's face, followed by a nip and pinch as geese dove to bite, slap, and claw, harrying them as they ran.

Chief and Pharaoh led Empress behind him.

Chief barked and growled at the geese. Jumping and swatting as he ran.

Sam and Pete took up their own firing positions in the rear.

After a stink cloud permeated the air, the geese fled, choking on the skunk's spray. "Yeah, you better run!" Sam called after them, laughing, but cut off with a cry because out of nowhere an angry pheasant ran directly into him, pecking his side.

"Hey, stop that," Pete called, warning, "I'll shoot if

you don't get away from him."

"You sprayed me and my mate while we were walking!" the pheasant clucked indignantly, ruffling his rich feathers.

Caesar ceased his run, spinning to see the pheasant backing away from Sam at its' mate's beckoning, though he continued his outraged cries. The geese were gone, and it looked like the battle was over. He surveyed his siblings and realized that the wet substance that had hit his face and speckled his siblings, was none other than goose poop.

Great, he thought sarcastically. Rubbing his cheek across a clump of wild grass before joining the others. The commotion had caused many animals to perk up out of dens or to cease their grazing.

Before long, antelope, deer, prairie dogs, squirrels, and even a few wild turkeys, came closer to watch the pheasant yell at a skunk.

"Hey, hey," Caesar cut in, coming to Sam's defense, and wanting to put an end to this. "You saw we were being attacked by geese. I promise Sam didn't spray you on purpose. He was just helping us get out of dodge."

"Caesar is right," a warm voice added, and they all looked to see the beaver River, and Buster the snake join them.

"River, is that you?" The pheasant paused.

"Yes, hello, Thomas. How is Maizie?" River said coming closer.

"Good—thank you," the pheasant said, in a much pleasanter voice. Looking to the side, he called over, "Maizie. Come over, dear. It's River!"

And soon the pheasant was joined by a hen.

"Does this guy know everybody around here?" Empress murmured to no one in particular.

It seemed that he did. Caesar was okay with it, though, if it meant that everyone would calm down. Enzo appeared out of nowhere, looking bedraggled.

"What happened to you?" Caesar asked.

The magpie grumbled, "One of the geese got me good, knocked me out of the air. I got caught in a bramble." He held up his wing to show that some of the feathers had prickly stickers poking out. He fluffed his wings, trying to shake them out.

"I can help with that," a tiny voice piped. And they looked to see a small chipmunk reaching up toward the bird.

"Thank you," Enzo replied, genuinely. "What's your name?"

"I'm Rocky. I saw everything from my tree. Why were those geese so mad?"

"Yes, why indeed?" The pheasant Thomas added,

while his wife nodded in agreement.

Caesar turned to see many eyes on him and the magpie. *I guess I'm the one doing the explaining*, he thought.

Caesar jumped up on a stone nearby to have a little higher advantage. The deer on the outskirts of the gathering were massive compared to him! Good thing they weren't meat eaters!

He barked in greeting and began to explain their mission and how they'd paused for lunch. They hadn't meant to upset the geese.

River and Enzo vouched for them, and soon, a gathering unlike any they had found themselves in before began. All the animals were uneasy after hearing of Razor, the coyotes, and their human captive.

Caesar could've sworn some of the animals rolled their eyes at the mention of Mona's name. *So, she didn't have all the animals' support,* he observed. Good!

As another day drew to a close, Caesar and his friends found themselves waving goodbye to River who, as was his custom, returned to his ferry to drift up and down river. He assured them that he'd warn everyone he met of Mona's betrayal and the dangers of Razor's ploys. He wished them luck and pushed off.

Enzo, having discussed it with the other animals, had decided they needed more support if they were ever going to take on Razor and the coyotes. He circled wide, scouted ahead, and cawed to all animals nearby to come to their gathering. By nightfall, Caesar was shocked to see dozens of various creatures littering the prairie. At first, they'd been worried that these animals would be on Mona's side, but Thomas and Maizie, the pheasants assured them, that none at this point and further east were with Mona—her bullying reputation preceded her.

But it was Buster the Bull Snake who came up with the plan.

CHAPTER 19

Laying down for bed that night, Caesar stared upwards at the stunning sky. Stars shined bright and he couldn't help but feel small. It was such a big world—universe! And here he was leading his siblings into danger. And yet, he felt like he was doing the right thing. Mom had always told him to protect the family, and Destiny was a part of that. They were going to find their girl and bring her home safely.

"Caesar," Empress whispered, sniffing and walking carefully toward him. "Is that you?"

He rose quickly, to help guide her around a cactus. "Hi," he said with a lick. "How are you doing?"

"Okay, I guess," she said, with a small laugh. "I've never wanted to go to the groomer more than this moment."

He smiled. He knew from experience that he and Empress both recoiled at the very mention. The place stunk like too many wet dogs. But he couldn't deny it. He was looking forward to a hot bath too.

"Do you think—" she began, but cut off, her chin dropping.

"What is it?" he asked her. This was unlike Empress. She was usually bold, sassy, and unafraid to speak her mind.

"Well, I... was just thinking that maybe you guys should leave me behind. I'm in the way," she concluded sadly.

"Empress, how can you say that? You're keeping up just as well as any of us," Caesar said reassuringly, but did wonder internally if perhaps she was right. Enzo had mentioned it before he left too. He wondered if she'd heard him.

The next day, according to Enzo and the numerous animals he'd gathered, would lead them to the bones. A hawk, though large and menacing, had sworn not to hunt within the area... shared how he'd seen the coyotes passing through, just earlier. It was dangerous, and Caesar wanted more than anything to keep Empress safe. And yet... he hesitated to split up. That mountain lion could still be out there. And whom would he leave behind with her?

"No, Empress, we do this together. We need you. You have great hearing and can sniff out our Cheeto girl," he said, trying to get her to smile. "Besides, somebody's gotta keep that puppy in line."

She cocked her head, "well, that's true," she admitted with a final sniffle. "My puppy does need me."

He smiled, thinking back to Chief who just earlier had fought off a mountain lion and then found food for everyone. But Caesar instead said, "yeah, you're right. He does need you looking after him."

Empress sniffed, trying to detect whether he was making fun of her or not, but then shook her head and spoke, "Thanks, Caesar. You're a really good brother."

His heart soared, and he gave her a quick reassuring nuzzle. "Let's get some sleep, okay? Tomorrow is gonna be a big day."

Caesar tossed and turned and finally, unable to sleep, got up to check the perimeter. Chief and Pharaoh dozed nearby. One of the puppy's eyelids opened slightly, but Caesar shook his head, and Chief fell back to sleep.

The night was still. Caesar could hear everything for what felt like miles. There were no cars or far off trains or planes, just calm. The quiet hum of nature. The running water yards off. The snores and sniffles of sleeping beasts. Caesar looked over his motley army. A pair of pheasant, a skunk, porcupine, turkeys, robins, a woodpecker, prairie dogs, chipmunks, squirrels, a duck, some antelope, a couple deer, a snake, and a few pets.

Enzo and River had taken off, claiming to go spread the word to get more helpers, and to scout ahead. Enzo in the sky and River along the waterways. But Caesar fretted. What if they were ditching them instead? What would happen if Mona caught up to them? What would happen tomorrow when they did run into the coyotes?

Being closer to the bones, it sounded—according to the hawk that had passed by with news—that Razor had slowed his pace, feeling confident that he would get Destiny to the location unchallenged.

"That won't happen," Caesar growled. The sun's rays weren't yet coming up, but he felt with a growing pit of unease that they'd better hurry. Without Enzo around, he decided it was his job to wake everyone.

"Okay, guys, let's—"

Before he could finish his wake-up call, something hit his head, and he was pulled down to the ground. He felt dizzy, a tiny mouse face appeared before him with a wicked grin. "Hello, Pet, thought you got away, didn't you!?" Mona squeaked, menacingly. Jerking her head to the side, to someone Caesar couldn't see, she ordered, "Take him."

Caesar wanted to protest or yell for help, but whatever had hit him made his head hurt and he fell unconscious.

CHAPTER 20

Destiny

For a summer evening, it was colder than she'd expected. Without a blanket—or pillow for that matter—sleeping was hard. There were no areas completely void of rocks or prickly plants. Shivering, Destiny sat up rubbing her arms. She had bruises and scrapes all over. Not to mention the bug bites. She'd been stung by a bee earlier on their march, but the owl hadn't let her stop to inspect it. She did so now, feeling at her ankle. The bump was there and hurt, but it wasn't crazy swollen like some pictures she'd seen in a science class. *Not allergic*, she thought gratefully.

Something crawled across her palm, and she

swatted at a large wolf spider creeping by. It scurried off into the darkness. "Ahhh," she shrieked, scooting over and rolling her shoulders in unease. She hated spiders! She sucked in air as she belatedly remembered the wounds on her upper back from the owl's talons. She stifled a sob, biting her lip, and looking around. A pair of eyes watched her in the blackness, and she knew the coyotes wouldn't let her escape.

Could she outrun them? she wondered. They weren't huge, but still, she'd seen one snap the neck of a rabbit in its jaws just hours ago. They would tear her a part. She shuddered at the thought. Her stomach growled loudly adding to her unease.

She watched as the coyote returned to surveying the area. She laid down to think, not wanting to draw any more attention to herself. She prayed the spider wasn't still there. *If only—*

"Psst."

Destiny's eyes widened, as she began to look around.

"Shhh, no, over here. Don't make a sound, Destiny."

Her jaw dropped, slightly. She hadn't told the coyotes or owl her name. They hadn't asked. *So, how could someone know it?*

Glancing around inconspicuously, she spied a dark yet illuminated spot near her head. Squinting, she asked, "Who?"

The spot moved closer, mere inches from her face. She tried not to gasp.

A bird appeared. A black and white bird. She recognized it as a magpie.

It came close and whispered, "I have news... Caesar is nearby. They're coming for you."

"What?" She asked, biting down her questions, and looking nervously in the direction of the coyote guard.

"Shh," the bird instructed.

She tried to steady her breathing. "He's here?" She whispered. "But how?"

The magpie lifted a wing as if to hush her. She clamped her mouth shut.

"You have to delay. You can't go where they're leading you... to the bones. If you do, your human world will be lost. Then, they'll kill you. Razor has been plotting this for some time, waiting until he could get a human child in his clutches."

"Bones?" she mumbled. A million questions ran through her head. She wanted to ask all of them, starting with how a tiny pomeranian had followed her here.

"The only thing keeping you alive right now is that you're needed for the bones. An old Native American place. Once that is done, the owl will give you to the coyotes," he whispered solemnly. "Do you understand?"

She exhaled, not entirely sure what he meant but knowing it wasn't good. "But what can I do?"

"Act sick. Go to the bathroom. Fall down. Cry! Humans do that a lot, right!? Whatever you can do to go slo-o-o-o-wly."

She nodded, but worried that it would only anger the evil owl more. She really didn't want him to drag her again by the shoulders, but... death... that was much worse. She bit her lip thinking.

"Caesar and the others are coming. You just need to stall."

"The others?" She asked, but before the bird could reply, a chorus of howls and yips sounded off. She sighed. It was her morning alarm.

The bird ruffled its feathers, whispering one final word, "Stall." And then he was gone.

Destiny slowly sat up, her mind a whirl. *The others?* He didn't mean that they'd all come, did he?

More howls interrupted her musing. Her eyes widened as she took in the new arrivals: wolves.

Her heart hammered in her chest. *How was she*

supposed to stall now?

Coyotes were scary, but wolves... the hulking beasts approaching were terrifying! She shivered as one growled menacingly and snapped its jaws with an audible click. Destiny let out an involuntary cry and flinched as the wolves swept past her.

You shouldn't have come, Caesar, she thought worriedly, wishing the bird was still there to warn off.

CHAPTER 21

It was the smell that got his attention first. It smelled like mouse poop... and bunny droppings too.

"Yuck," Caesar choked out, trying to sit up, before he remembered the events of last night.

He tugged and found that all four of his legs were bound. His nose quivered, taking in all the smells. It was dark. He was inside somewhere.... Or something. *Am I dead?* He thought. *Was I eaten and don't remember?* He frantically tried to look around.

"Shhhhhhh," a voice soothed. "Don't make a s-s-s-s-sound."

"Buster?" Caesar asked, his pulse rising.

"Yes-s-s-s-s," the voice sounded pleased to be recognized.

Out of the darkness, a flame appeared. Mona held one lit match before her.

Caesar growled in his throat. They were in a cave, and he was—to his dismay—surrounded by a horde of mice, rabbits, a large bull snake, and other vermin. The cave reeked like excrement and fungi.

A beetle scurried nearby Caesar's face, and before he had time to react, the bull snake lunged for it, eating it in one bite.

Caesar cried out in startlement.

"Shut up, Pet," Mona commanded, coming closer, match gripped in tiny paw.

"What do you want, Mona?" Caesar spat angrily, trying—and failing—to escape his bonds.

Buster hissed at him warningly.

Caesar growled, "You're a traitor. What about River?"

The snake peered at him with its creepy eyes. "River is my friend, but this-s-s-s-s... is-s-s-s too good an opportunity to mis-s-s-s-s."

"We sent Buster ahead. When he didn't return from his scouting, we knew he must have found something. So, we floated the river."

"But how? You're mice... what did you float on?" Caesar couldn't help it. He'd always been a curious pup.

"We've smuggled in some human goods over the years. An innertube does quite nicely," Mona gloated.

Caesar laughed. "And you call me 'pet!' Look at you, with your matches and innertube. You love the human zone, whether you want to admit or not. What will you do once you can't cross over and take their things?"

Mona only glared, "We will be just fine."

Caesar didn't miss the glance Buster gave Mona. "Don't snakes eat mice?"

"And pocket pets too," Mona squeaked, continuing, "Besides, Buster and I have a deal. He doesn't eat mice or bunnies on this side, in exchange for information. Birds and prairie dogs though? Have at them." She nodded at someone outside of Caesar's vision.

A slap.

"Hey, ouch. Stop that." Caesar craned his neck to see, and he glimpsed tufts of white and black fur, with the smell of rabbit. "Bilbo," Caesar growled. "Another traitor."

"The only traitor around here is you… and your other pets. We need that girl to lift the bones and seal the animal zone forever. We can't have you interfering," the military mouse snapped.

"But—"

Another slap.

Caesar growled. He would kill that two-timing bunny! He craned his neck, glaring at Bilbo.

The bunny didn't say anything, his ears were flat against his head, and he avoided Caesar's gaze while following Mona's commands.

Caesar growled louder as the bunny pummeled his furry body.

This time the snake lunged coming mere inches from the pomeranian's face. "Mona promis-s-s-s-sed me if you become too unruly, I can eat you for breakfas-s-s-s-t."

Caesar trembled, involuntarily.

"Enough," Mona ordered. "We're wasting daylight. We must break camp. And you," she held the match closer. "You're coming with us."

CHAPTER 22

Trudging along the rugged terrain, surrounded by rabbits, mice, and a treacherous bull snake, Caesar grumbled to himself. *How did they sneak up on him? What about his siblings? Who would watch over Empress? And what about Destiny?* He prayed Chief didn't do anything stupid.

"Can you at least tell me where you're taking me?"

Mona's whiskers quivered as she walked beside him. She looked like she was thinking about it. He eyed her hopefully.

She spun around, "It's like this, kid… you're the bait. Once that girl lifts the bones, we'll offer you to

Razor and the coyotes as a prize, to make them stall... and then... we'll pounce and eliminate them."

"You're going to try and kill coyotes? But you're smaller than I am! And what happens to me then?"

She laughed wickedly, her whiskers shaking with her mirth. "We're tougher than we look. We'll take out their legs first. And...," she paused as if for effect, "You'll have done your part by then. You'll be dead."

"I get any scraps-s-s-s-s-s," Buster added.

Caesar couldn't hide his dismay.

"Besides, we have friends coming. The only ones who will be dead is you and that human of yours... and the owl, of course." The mouse scampered ahead, her laughter cutting off as she called out commands.

Caesar surveyed the area. There were bunnies and mice everywhere! He could probably outrun them, couldn't he? They had removed his bindings once they started their march eastward toward the bones. He needed a distraction.

As it stood, if his siblings kept on their track, three parties would arrive separately to the bones. Which would be first though, was the question.

He needed to get away from these jerks and get to Destiny. As he racked his brain for possibilities, he suddenly heard a gurgled cry!

And then his eyes went huge!

Around him, mice and rabbits were fleeing from an aerial assault. The scene was utter chaos. A mouse was lifted in the air by a talon, another lobbed into a bunny. Neither Mona nor Bilbo were anywhere to be seen.

"Run, Caesar," a familiar voice cawed.

It was Enzo! How he had found him, and how he'd been able to summon an air force of pigeons, crows, and even some northern flicker woodpeckers, Caesar didn't ask. He just obeyed and started to run.

"Not s-s-s-so fas-s-s-s-st!" The snake lashed out toward Caesar, but the pomeranian was quick. And he hopped out of the snake's reach, darting down the prairie. Toward Destiny with a flock of birds at his back.

Spirits lifting, he barked his thanks, as Enzo cawed and led the way, the glorious sunrise lighting his path!

After running for what seemed like an hour, Enzo led Caesar to a small creek where he could quench his thirst. Many of the birds had scattered after the attack, going ahead to warn Caesar's siblings and to gather more support. The main battle between Razor and the coyotes was about to begin.

"How did you know where I was?" Caesar asked the magpie.

Enzo cawed as if offended. "I have my ways," he said mischievously. "And besides, that's not important, I've spoken to Destiny."

"WHAT!?" Caesar leapt up from the creek, spinning around as if she might appear out of thin air. "Where? Is she okay?"

"Listen," Enzo said, in an exasperated tone. "They're near the bones. I told her to stall in any way that she can."

"We have to go then!" Caesar barked. "Lead the way."

"Upon your word," Enzo said formally, nodding his head before lifting into the air. "Your siblings aren't too far off either. We'll meet with them—and their forces, and together, approach the bones. Our mission to preserve the human zone still has a chance!"

CHAPTER 23

After another few minutes, Caesar's ear perked up. The mice and rabbits hadn't been able to carry him too far off, but in the time he'd been unconscious, his siblings had continued on. And now, blessedly, he could hear his sister's annoying whining. It was music to his ears!

He barked to announce his presence, and then crested the hill to see them gathered below, still among their diverse party of creatures. Chief was the first to notice. He barked and charged up the hillside to greet Caesar.

"Puppy! Where are you going?" Empress cried.

Caesar saw Pharaoh lean in to explain, and heard

her follow up with, "Caesar, what were you thinking going on ahead without us?"

He sighed. Maybe 'music to his ears' wasn't exactly the right way to put it.

"Brother, where were you? I smelled something else besides your scent, but Empress wouldn't let me go look for you. 'She said you were stubborn and trying to be the hero.'"

Caesar sighed again, but at Chief's crestfallen face, he rushed to reassure him. "You did the right thing, it's okay, Chief. I'm back. Let's go down so I can tell the others too."

Chief, though huge, bent down to rub his nose against Caesar's and waited for him to pass before following. It made Caesar feel an odd mix of pride and embarrassment. Enzo said he was the "alpha" of the pack. Caesar didn't think of himself like that... and yet, as he looked at his siblings and new friends who awaited him, he did feel a responsibility over them. *Is that what being the alpha meant?*

After spending a few moments explaining what had happened, Caesar attempted to calm Empress down. She was in hysterics, muttering her desire to squash that stupid mouse while also profusely apologizing. Both moods unsettled Caesar. He had to stop her chewing on her front paw before she did any damage.

"It's alright. Seriously, I'm okay. But... we have to be careful. Buster betrayed us..." he looked at them and spoke softer, "we don't know who we can trust here."

Enzo hopped down to stand on Pharaoh's large-shelled back.

Pharaoh cleared his throat, but it didn't deter the bird.

Caesar eyed him. He truly believed they could trust the magpie, and the porcupine and skunk boys who were fidgeting just outside their circle. But the others? His eyes took in the antelope, prairie dogs, other birds, the grumpy pheasant, and more.

"We need an oath from everyone that their motives are pure and that they are committed to stopping Razor and saving Destiny. If they can't do that, we don't want them with us." Caesar wasn't sure how Enzo would respond. The bird cocked his head at him, as if thinking about it.

"If you insist, Caesar, but we must hurry."

"It'll go fast. Gather everyone," Caesar barked.

As the bird flew off squawking instructions, Empress yipped approval. "Wow, Caesar. This place has changed you. You're... tough here."

Caesar's momentary smile turned into a frown as

she continued, "Don't let it get to your head though. I'm still taking your bed once we're back home."

Sigh.

The vows took only a few moments. Enzo made a great speech reminding everyone of their purpose. Razor and his coyote gang are trying to commit animal zone treason by not only bringing a human into the land but by attempting to move the sacred bones. Razor has to be stopped. The human needs to be rescued and delivered to the pets so they can see her safely back to her own zone. If anyone doesn't like it, they can leave.

Beyond a couple squirrels and a lone marmot, all others agreed.

As the final creature uttered the vow, hoofbeats thundered nearby.

Caesar barked in alarm to get everyone's attention, but Enzo cawed merrily. "They came!"

Caesar looked at him in confusion as a herd of wild horses appeared. They came in varying shades: blacks, browns, whites, buckskin, and speckled. They were... "stunning," Caesar mumbled aloud. He had seen horses before, some of their neighbors back in Molt had them. But these... *these* were powerful, wild creatures.

"They're on our side, right?" Pharaoh asked, sounding uneasy. Those hooves would do damage to all of them if not.

"Of course, they are!" Enzo cried. "I sent word to them that Razor was nearing the bones."

"My name is Goes Ahead," a large black stallion neighed from the front. "We will run with you!"

Caesar's breath caught at the mighty voice and rippling muscles under a gleaming coat. Caesar noticed his friends all looked mesmerized too. All, except Chief.

Chief barked happily and ran ahead. "Goes Ahead! It's me, Chief!"

Caesar thought his tongue had fallen out. Before he could warn him to be careful, his huge yet little brother ran right up to the lead horse. And to their surprise, Goes Ahead bent his great head to nuzzle the dog's!

"They know each other?" Empress whispered tersely; no doubt frustrated she couldn't see what was happening.

"Welcome, little brother. Let us run together once more!"

And just like that, they took off! The hooves thundering on ahead, birds taking to the air, and the tiny, tailed creatures trying to keep up. Chief ran merry circles around them all, barking encouragingly.

Caesar and his siblings stood only for a moment more, before Caesar barked orders, and Chief returned to help lead Empress. However possible, it seemed Chief had grown up here in the animal zone. So, how had he been discovered on the human side? It was a great mystery, but Caesar set it aside for now. For the first time in days, he felt extremely hopeful. With the horses, the coyotes wouldn't stand a chance!

CHAPTER 24

Destiny

"Get up, you worthless human!" The owl screeched at her, digging his talons into her shoulders as he had done before, reopening her wounds.

Destiny cried out in pain but didn't get up. "I can't," she wailed. The magpie had told her to stall, and stall, she would. Her life depended on it. Even if it meant the flesh of her shoulders was being ripped apart.

She sat on the ground, cradling her ankle. She had improvised and pretended to trip over a knotted root, feigning that she'd twisted her ankle. Now that the enormous bird was attacking her, her cries of pain were no longer acting. Her shoulders felt like they were on fire.

"You get up, or I'll have them drag you there!" The owl snapped. "Samson," Razor cried, and his coyote sidekick approached, tongue lolling at the side—from fatigue or anticipation of a meal, Destiny couldn't tell.

She shuddered looking him over. Samson was the biggest of the coyotes, and the meanest. He'd attacked a smaller one just yesterday for being too slow. Coyotes from all around had heard the nightly yips and howls, and their numbers had grown to over thirty. Now with the wolves in team, their numbers must have been fifty or more.

Destiny didn't know how Caesar—or her—could ever expect to defeat them. She bit her lip and stifled a cry, as the owl released her. She could feel warm blood trickling down her back from the ragged wounds.

And yet, she sat with tears streaking her face while cradling her foot. It was her only chance. She had tried to gag herself when no one was looking but... someone was always looking! The coyotes and wolves were everywhere. A hurt ankle was the only act she could think of.

"Get up," Samson snarled, licking his lips, as his menacing eyes looked her up and down as if she were an upcoming meal.

She gulped, but stayed where she was.

If the magpie was telling the truth, the owl needed her to move some bones—creepy! But after that, he'd be done with her.

They were bluffing. They couldn't kill her yet. But... she eyed the large coyote's teeth as he stood snarling at her. They could hurt her.

"Okay," she said softly. "I'll try, but I can't go as fast," she added, beginning to stand up. She feigned a limp. The coyote snapped, and she screamed as his teeth bit into her forearm.

"Then I'll drag you," Samson growled still locked onto her arm, just before dropping it roughly.

She clutched her now bleeding arm to her chest, momentarily forgetting her shoulder pain.

"That's enough, Samson," Razor said in his cool voice, circling overhead. "I'm sure the human understands your message. Don't you?" he said, directing his attention toward Destiny.

"Yes," she sobbed, her arm stinging terribly. She was struggling to do anything but breathe through the pain.

The owl watched her expectantly, and she knew she had to reply, or Samson would come at her again.

"I'll walk," she mumbled.

"See that you do. It doesn't take two arms to lift the bones." The owl took to the air and hooted ominously, "the bones are just over the next hill. And then your work here will be done."

Samson snickered, flicking his tail as he turned his back on her to command the rest of his gang: "Move out."

Destiny limped on as the coyotes swarmed close to urge her onward, her heart slamming in her chest. *What now?*

CHAPTER 25

"I smell something," Empress said, nose twitching as they walked. She turned her head left and right as she walked in between Pharaoh and Chief. Caesar just in front. They had decided not to try and tether her to Chief's back anymore in case Chief needed to move quickly and fight. He could better protect Empress that way.

Caesar sniffed deeply in response to Empress's statement. He smelled lots of things. Trees. Plants. Dirt. Flowers. Animal droppings. Nature smells were everywhere.

Sniff sniff sniff.

"Don't you smell that? It's—"

Sniff. Sniff sniff sniffffffffff.

"It's—" SNIFF. "It's her!" Empress barked triumphantly. Nose wriggling in rapidly.

Caesar looked at his sister. "Are you sure?" He sniffed, still not picking up on anything.

Her nose was rooted in the ground examining a knot in the soil.

"Is that... blood?" Pharaoh asked soberly.

Caesar's pulse spiked, and he leapt back to inspect what Empress sniffed at.

He sniffed deeply, and to his utter astonishment—and dismay—found that his sister was right. It was Destiny. One of her hairs was lying on the ground near droplets of now dried blood.

"She's hurt," he whispered.

"She's been here," Empress said, dramatics aside. "I can smell her. Come on, boys!" she barked, picking up the pace. "Someone tell those horses we need to veer north!"

Caesar eyed his sister momentarily. Her loss of sight had enhanced her other senses. Her sense of smell and hearing were her superpowers. He was impressed!

"Go tell them, Enzo," Caesar barked up at the magpie who flew ahead.

Sam and Pete hurried up near them. "We're

close?" Pete the porcupine asked.

"We're close," Caesar confirmed. "Good luck," he told them, as they nodded and ran ahead to take their positions. Caesar worried of their seemingly carefree attitude.

"You can't protect everyone, Caesar. They know the risks and yet came... as did we," Pharaoh told him as if reading his mind.

"I know, Pharaoh. I just worry."

"And that's why we look to you, brother. We know you have our best interest at heart." The large reptile told him.

Caesar smiled at him, thinking back to what Pharaoh had shared. He was much older than they'd known and had lived a whole other life with his first owner. For some reason, his trust in Caesar meant all the more because of it.

Just then a horse neighed, signaling for them to stop. Caesar snapped his attention on Goes Ahead who trotted over, Enzo perched on his back.

"We've spotted them," Goes Ahead announced. "They are circling the bones now. We have to hurry. Are you prepared, Tiny Tail?"

Tiny Tail? Caesar paused. In another time, this nickname would've been hard to swallow. Now, coming from this majestic stallion, Caesar felt nothing but pride. "I am. I mean, we are," he replied, trying to sound as brave as possible.

Enzo cawed his approval.

"Then we ride—NOW!" Goes Ahead neighed, spun around, and cantered back to the herd. The wild horses—ten in number—split into two groups and tore off down the hill. One side to the left, the other to the right to try and encircle the coyotes. That left a dead-straight path for Caesar and the others to cut to Destiny.

Caesar barked, and the birds, antelope, deer, skunk, porcupine, and others ran full speed ahead, followed by one massive puppy and one tiny pomeranian.

"Be careful, Caesar," Empress called, having been ordered to stay behind with Pharaoh. They were to keep watch—literally and figuratively—and send birds out as messengers if anyone got away. A score of pigeons, robins, and doves awaited their orders while perched atop the nearby trees.

Empress hadn't been pleased at first, but after Goes Ahead agreed, she dropped it. Who could argue with him?

"I love you both!" Caesar called over his shoulder with a final glance in their direction, praying it wouldn't be the last time he saw them.

He could see Empress quivering, leaning into Pharaoh, as he whispered to her comfortingly.

They'll be alright, Caesar told himself. They had to be. But now, he had to pay attention. He was headed into battle.

CHAPTER 26

Dust flew, horses whinnied, and the coyotes howled, but one sound cut through the din—the cries of a lone human.

"Destiny!" Caesar barked. He couldn't see anything. Skunk spray permeated the air and mixed with the dust. He couldn't smell anything definitive either. He was isolated. Surrounded by enemies and allies, and yet, unable to get his bearings.

"Caesar, look out!" Chief barked, hurdling over a fallen sapling and slamming into a snarling coyote mere inches from Caesar.

Caesar jumped aside just in time to watch his brother close his jaws around the coyote's neck, snapping it as he shook ferociously. The tiny pomeranian couldn't believe it. *Chief? The big puppy... a warrior?*

The large dog let the corpse fall from his jaws, kicking it with finality. "Let's go!" he barked, paving a path down the middle.

Caesar stayed right behind him, as they'd planned.

The skunk and porcupine could be heard just ahead shouting, "Shoot" and "fire."

But throughout the chaos, Destiny's screams made Caesar's blood go cold. "Where is Destiny? Can you see her?"

Before Chief could respond, a horse cut in front of them pursued by a pack of—

"Wolves," Chief growled.

Wolves! Caesar wondered, aghast. *Where had they come from?* Mona had said all the major predators kept to the mountains. But there had been the mountain lion. So, apparently, she hadn't had all the facts right.

The wolves ran down the horse, and its shrieks filled the air as it was overwhelmed by the force.

Caesar gasped as he watched the wolves slay the poor beast.

Another horse whinnied behind them, and Caesar barely avoided being trampled by the angry herd. Goes Ahead bore down on the wolves and scattered them, stomping on one and kicking another as he ran to his comrade's rescue.

Caesar stood frozen. He was only a four-pound house pet! He shouldn't be out here!

He watched in terror as Chief battled a large lone wolf in front of him. Chief growled and battered the wolf, who in return slashed his teeth against Chief's front leg. The puppy howled in pain but did not cease his battering.

Caesar was helpless. "Chief!" he cried.

Suddenly, white and black feathers obscured his view. A bird tugged on his fur. "Caesar, run! You can't help them. The horses will deal with the wolves. You have to get to Destiny," Enzo cawed.

Caesar looked from his brother, who had successfully beaten off the wolf, as a horse came to kick at it. Chief was safe for the moment. Another scream sliced through the air.

Destiny. Caesar didn't hesitate any longer. She was the reason he'd come, and he was going to get his girl to safety, even if it killed him!

"Enzo, get our troops!" Caesar barked and tore off dodging and diving, eluding the evil canines' snapping jaws. Though tiny, he was fast and determined. Mom had told him to look after Destiny, so that's what he was going to do.

Amidst the swirling dust, fighting figures, and screams, howls, and yips, he located which direction Destiny's voice was coming from. He caught up to Sam and Pete, who had done a fantastic job of clearing a path while the horses sectioned groups of coyotes and wolves off to fight.

There, down the center and near a large Ponderosa Pine, an evil owl dragged Destiny by its talons. Judging by her anguished expression, she was in pain, and that made the pomeranian furious.

"Get away from her!" Caesar barked, leaping into action. He jumped over a sage plant, skidded around one coyote that was engaged with a wolf, of all things, and narrowly missed being kicked by Harmony, the buckskin mare and Goes Ahead's mate who had made it the furthest of all the horses. She battled many coyotes and wolves by herself! Goes Ahead's hooves thundered as he hastened to help her.

The owl hadn't heard Caesar, but he was about to!

"I SAID, 'GET AWAY FROM HER!'" Caesar emitted, an ear-splitting sound. The owl momentarily swiveled his head around, releasing Destiny as he did so. She sagged to her knees.

"Get down, Destiny!" Caesar barked. He wasn't sure if she could hear him or not, but she did in fact fall into a cradled position.

"Now Pete!"

The Porcupine had quills in reserve for this exact purpose. He stopped running, squatted, and fired!

The owl screeched as quills flew through the air in his direction. Razor flew back a few yards, giving enough room for Sam, Pete, Caesar, and Enzo to surround Destiny. She was breathing...that was good. However, the blood stains visible on her tattered shirt heightened Caesar's anger.

Goes Ahead stomped over, claw marks visible down one side, but otherwise unhurt, as was his mate. The other horses gathered nearby the pair. Most of the coyotes and wolves had left their dead and retreated, gathering to lick their wounds—or to strike out one last time together.

Caesar was just about to tell Destiny to get on Goes Ahead when a squeaky voice cut through the air.

"Now, wait just a minute, Pet."

Mona the mouse. She was alive! And—

"Let go of me," Empress cried.

Caesar's blood chilled just as he looked up to see Mona, Bilbo, and Buster, and their mouse and rabbit horde. They had taken Empress and Pharaoh captive. Mona stood pointing a quill, one she had most likely picked up after Pete's last shot and held it mere inches from Empress's eye. The bull snake had looped its body around Pharaoh and held its jaws above his neck.

"Move and your friends die!" Mona called, laughing. Turning back toward the owl who flew above surveying the new arrivals. "You must be Razor," Mona squeaked. "I have a proposition for you."

CHAPTER 27

"Well, well, what do we have here?" the wicked owl hooted, hovering over the fray.

Caesar felt ice in his veins. Destiny lay injured, Empress and Pharaoh had been captured, and he had left Chief to fight wolves—alone. He was no protector. He had failed. He—

"Caesar, don't listen to them! You get our girl and go!"

It was Empress. Dramatic, feisty, blind as a bat Empress. The bravest, greatest sister he could ever ask for!

"Shut up, or I'll kill you!" Mona screeched, quill quivering closer toward Empress's eye.

Caesar barked angrily as Bilbo kicked Empress. She didn't even yelp. She, as only she could do— even while captured—lifted her chin haughtily, seemingly unfazed.

"Enough!" The owl cried. "Speak, mouse, or I'll make a meal out of you." He paused, head swiveling. "My pack will be hungry after all of this... activity."

Caesar spun to see figures emerging as the dust settled. The horses whinnied, spinning and raking their hooves through the prairie floor, preparing to charge again. They were down to eight horses. The remainder of Caesar's forces had fallen back. What hope could turkeys, antelope, or pheasants have with wolves?

Sam and Pete looked forlorn, and even Enzo hopped from foot to foot nervously on Goes Ahead's back.

Destiny stirred, moaning softly.

Caesar was torn. Did he stay with her or rush to protect his siblings?

"It's like this," the mouse began. "These pets are human lovers. They came looking for... her," the mouse pointed with the quill before repositioning it at Empress's head. "I offer them to you. All I ask is that if we agree to let you use the human to lift the bones, you swear like Buster has, to not eat the prairie mice or rabbits."

A low voice snarled from nearby, "Ha! You expect us to agree? Rabbits are my favorite!" A huge hulking coyote purred as he approached from behind Mona, snapping his jaws for affect.

Mona squeaked, and Bilbo made to run but was caught by the coyote.

"Hold on, Samson," Razor hooted, dropping to perch on the tree.

Caesar could see the bones of a large bison, a rack of antlers, and an eagle feather beside the tree—just as he'd heard about.

"You ask a lot of us, mouse. We can take the pets... and still eat you too."

A snarled howl reverberated in the air just as a horse shrieked. Another had been taken down by the pack of wolves and coyotes.

Caesar knew then they had lost.

"Okay, okay, take the rabbits. I don't care about them but spare the mice. If you do that, we'll work with you. I have an extensive network which spans the entire prairie. Save the mice, and you'll never go hungry again. They can sniff out any creature you wish. Take him as an offering," she gestured toward Bilbo, who glowered at her.

"Traitor," the trapped bunny groaned.

Razor cocked his head, measuring her. "Deal," he hooted. "Now, someone get that human. She must move the bones before any other delays."

As he spoke, chaos broke out.

Caesar barked, "Get up, Destiny. You have to wake up. You have to run!"

"Caesar," she whispered, looking up, tears streaking her face. "I—I thought I was imagining it. You're really here?"

Caesar licked her nose affectionately, "Yes, now get up, don't let them—"

"Move, pet," the large coyote snarled, swatting his paw, sending Caesar flying.

Destiny screamed again as the coyote's jaws tightened around her forearm and began dragging her. She sobbed, crawling attempting to stand, but before she could, a form blurred by.

Chief swiped his large paws down the unsuspecting coyote's face. Samson howled as the dog's claws raked his eye. Snarling and lashing out, the coyote rolled, which caused Chief to stumble. The coyote growled for Destiny to move.

Forms emerged, having fought off the horses who now were cut off from the bones. Between the now seven horses and the bones was a large pack of frothing and angry coyotes and wolves. Caesar, seemingly forgotten about, momentarily met eyes with Enzo, who chattered with alarm nearby.

Empress and Pharaoh were still under threat. Destiny was alive—for now. Chief regained his footing and prepared to launch at Samson.

Caesar took the opportunity to rush Mona, who had dropped the quill and was beginning to back away. Enzo cawed, "NOW!" He flew right at Buster's head, pecking at the snake's eye while Caesar pounced on Mona. He held the tiny mouse down while Enzo, aided by Sam and Pete, were able to dislodge the snake from Pharaoh. Having scooped up the quill, Sam held it in his teeth and pressed it to the snake's throat. "Move and we'll kill you, traitor," Sam growled.

Caesar glared down at Mona, who didn't even squirm. She only... laughed. "You? Really? You expect me to believe that you're going to kill me? You're just a pet. You don't belong out here. You don't have what it takes to be a killer."

Before he could bark his response though, Destiny shrieked.

Apparently, Razor had grown tired of waiting. While Samson and Chief still battled, the owl had swept in once again, renewing his purpose to drag the human girl toward the bones.

At the commotion, Caesar had jumped, only to find Mona gone. "Crap," he grumbled. He had let her escape. But none of that mattered right now. Sam and Pete were with Empress and Pharaoh. They were safe for the moment, but not if Razor got Destiny to lift the bones.

The owl hooted angrily. "Do it now! Lift them."

Her feet stood on the edge of the skeleton. Razor released her, causing her to collapse to her knees just before the bison bones. All around went still as every creature turned to watch the human's next move. The light breeze tickled the eagle feather that sprouted from buck antler's laying near scattered bison bones. It waved ever so lightly.

"Destiny, NO!" Caesar barked. But he was too late. She raised her hands just above the bones preparing to lift them.

"YES," the owl hooted wickedly. "DO IT NOW!" His evil laughter wiping out all other sounds.

They had lost, Caesar realized, a pit forming in his stomach.

CHAPTER 28

Everything flashed before Caesar's eyes. Empress who now stood crying and trembling in fear, once arriving home swaddled in a pink blanket. The shelled Pharaoh standing helpless yet stoically once arriving home with Mom, head tucked in nervously. Chief, the giant puppy, who lay on his side breathing heavily with a bloodied leg as the coyotes closed in, once dancing around the dinner table happily thwacking his tail into everyone and everything. And Destiny, who knelt bloody and broken before the bones, once sitting on the kitchen floor scratching behind Caesar's ears and smelling of Cheetos.

It had been a perfect life. Their life together. They were a family. And... and Caesar blinked. He couldn't let it end like this.

He shook his head to clear it, and barked, dashing around figures and friends as he called to Destiny. "Destiny, I'm coming. Don't listen to him. Don't touch the bones!"

Destiny, hands raised mere inches away from the bones and feather, paused looking toward Caesar. Or rather, beyond Caesar. As he barked and ran toward her, the ground began to tremble. The cloudy sky broke with a pocket of sunshine bursting forth. As Caesar ran it seemed that many others joined him. The owl lifted quickly to the air, looking at Caesar.

"What is he doing? Someone get that pet! What is he doing?" the owl hooted with alarm.

The ground thundered as if it were an earthquake. And in a way, it was.

For just as Destiny hovered over the bones, and Caesar cleared the last obstacle, he made it to her and jumped in her lap licking and kissing and pleading for her to back away. As he did, voices boomed from all around. Dozens. Hundreds. A multitude of voices.

"What is he doing?" The owl screeched, hovering in the air, but was cut off as eagles appeared through in the sunshine clawing and screeching as they tore him apart. The owl flew off but was taken down almost instantly by the eagles who soared above.

And from seemingly all around, the coyote and wolf howls were cut off as they were trampled by the massive bison which thundered onto the scene.

Destiny gasped and clutched Caesar tight. Sam, Pete, and Pharaoh quickly ushered Empress over to them. Horses whinnied triumphantly as the remaining warriors were joined in battle.

Enzo squawked, "Caesar, look!" He was perched on the tree and as the group looked, they saw Razor, what was left of him, drop to the ground as the eagles swept over the battlefield in large swooping arcs and screeching their victory.

"No," Enzo cawed, "Look there! It's River!"

Caesar looked again and was shocked to see a single beaver clutching some sort of reins around a bull bison's mighty neck.

"Would you look at that?" Pharaoh murmured, holding his neck outstretched to see.

"We won!" Sam and Pete cried in unison. Jumping and whooping with celebration.

"Not yet, you didn't," a voice snarled, as Samson the coyote, blood dripping from his now blind eye, jumped for them.

Destiny screamed, throwing Caesar behind her, throwing her arms up to stave off the brunt of his attack.

"No," Caesar yelled as he helplessly watched the brute's jaws going for her throat.

Empress screamed in terror.

A blur leapt over the bones, knocking Destiny to the ground, and slamming into Samson. It was Chief. His front leg was bleeding badly, and there were tendrils of blood across his coat. But in that instant, he was nothing of the puppy Caesar had known.

He was a warrior. He was a wild thing raised in this rugged land. A descendant of a powerful and sacred people whose connection to the earth and animals was long.

Chief pounced on Samson and with one final twist, he snapped the wretched coyote's neck between his jaws.

Breathing heavily, he turned slowly to look them over. He nodded at Caesar and his siblings, and then to Destiny, "You are safe."

"I... but... why—" Destiny spluttered. But before she could say anything Chief collapsed beside the bones, feathers, slain coyote, and the human who had despised him since the day she had met him.

CHAPTER 29

"I knew you'd come through!" Enzo told River.

"Absolutely. Did everything go okay? Where's Buster?" The beaver asked, glancing around. He had come to stand with the group, having jumped off the lead bull's back after the fighting had ended.

"The traitor you mean?" Empress sniffed. "I told you I don't like snakes, with good reason!"

Enzo nodded, as River glanced at him, chattering, "It's true, he was an agent of Mona's."

"Really?" River asked, appearing genuinely shocked. "I—," he paused looking at the group. "I'm so sorry. I had no idea. Where is he?"

"He got away, when you all arrived. We were holding him down, but as soon as the bison appeared we got out of dodge." Sam explained, sheepishly.

"You don't mean this snake, do you?"

The group spun around to see Bilbo and a team of rabbits sitting on the snake, one pressing a quill, just as Sam had done earlier, at his neck.

"That'd be the one," River said, walking toward the snake, and shaking his head with disappointment.

Buster wriggled nervously as the angry beaver approached, "I'll take it from here, boys."

Caesar watched as River signaled to one of the eagles to take the snake. The bird commanded utter obedience from the snake, who went still at its words. The eagle flew off the snake in tow. Once out of sight, Caesar heard later that the snake was dropped. He would have to journey a very far distance before ever making his way back here.

The remaining bison and eagles settled around, mourning the lost horses, and pushing the treacherous coyote, wolf, and owl remains aside. They did not deserve the honor of burial or mourning. They were traitors to the sacred bones, as per the bull, Boulder, who led the bison herd.

His massive head with tufts of fuzzy brown hair and horns bowed to Caesar.

Caesar, suddenly feeling the urge to go potty, kept his composure—just barely—in front of the intimidating and powerful Boulder.

"You may be from the other side, but here we honor all warriors, especially those who fight to protect our sacred bones and way of life. Thank you, tiny but mighty, Caesar—and companions. We wish you a safe journey home and will aid you however we can."

"Not so fast," a tiny voice squeaked.

Caesar spun, gasping to see Mona the military mouse standing on the bones, tiny paw tugging at the feather.

"If she's not gonna do it, then I will!" She cried shrilly.

Boulder snorted angrily stamping his foot, but before he charged, a black and white bird swept overhead, grabbing the unsuspecting mouse, and soared upwards. As the magpie rose in the air, he dropped her. Her scream was suddenly cut off as an eagle snatched her with its beak, killing her instantly.

"Sacred child, you have been treated terribly. You must have questions. Yet, you are so quiet."

Caesar looked over sadly to where Destiny now sat cradling Chief's head in her lap. She looked up, tears streaming down her face.

"I was terrible to him," she whispered. "I was so mean. I hated him. And still... he saved me."

Boulder's huge head bowed, "Chief, was a valiant warrior. Known by many in this land as a guardian of the bones."

"But how?" Empress cried. She sat near them, nuzzling Chief's limp body. Though they had tied some of Destiny's torn shirt around his leg wound, he had lost a lot of blood and fallen unconscious. His heartbeat slowing, he appeared lifeless.

"He's my puppy," Empress sobbed. "He wasn't supposed to die here. How could he be from here? He's not dead, right? Puppy?" She pleaded, rubbing her nose across Chief's limp arm. "You're still with us, aren't you, Chief? Wake up, puppy. I'll help you. You just have to wake up."

Tears spilled from Caesar as he watched his sister unable to accept the loss of their brother. He stepped forward to comfort her, but then a hush fell across the prairie.

Soon, whispers broke out from all—bison included—and many backed away. The eagles landed, bowing their heads.

"Whoa," Pharaoh mumbled, tucking his head reverently.

Caesar, being shorter, couldn't see anything, and soon he found himself standing alone near his human and canine sisters, along with his brother's fallen body.

"Chief was found near this place on the human side. We brought him here for a time, with his littermates until they were big enough to return to the human zone." A low, rich voice spoke.

Destiny turned and gasped.

Caesar did as well.

"What in the heck is happening?" Empress squeaked.

Standing before them was a giant buck, the largest Caesar had ever seen, and gleaming white.

"The albino deer," Sam mumbled reverently.

"It's true," Pete added, equally stunned.

An albino deer, indeed, Caesar thought, trembling from the overwhelming presence and magnitude of this moment. Eagles, bison, and an albino deer— leading a score of regular coated deer behind, all had eyes on the tiny pomeranian.

"My name is White Cloud," the deer introduced.

Caesar quickly regained his wits and introduced himself and his siblings. Destiny still held Chief's head possessively and Empress buried her face in his matted, bloodied coat.

White Cloud approached them, and Empress and Destiny only hesitated for a moment. No one could deny this creature's mighty presence. Slowly, Destiny stood up, grimacing with the effort; the horse Goes Ahead stepped over to support her. His mate Harmony nuzzled her cheek.

And so it was, when all hope had failed, and dusk began to fall, that an albino deer tipped his massive antlers to touch the giant puppy, whispering softly in his ear.

Caesar and the others bent their heads, thinking it a moment of mourning.

"Wh—what happened?" A voice croaked.

"Chief," Destiny and Caesar gasped aloud—as Empress crooned, "MY PUPPY!"

"But how?" Destiny asked turning to the deer, as Empress nuzzled and laughed at Chief, ordering him not to move, her usual flood of maternal lecturing renewed.

"He was dead," Destiny stated.

"He was *near* death," the deer replied. "There's a difference."

"But... how?" Caesar asked, joining in the conversation. "Did you use magic?"

The deer laughed, a deep yet melodic trill. "Magic, not I. I only reminded him of his duty."

"And what's that?" Destiny asked.

"To find his tribe and remain with them. Maybe he was only sleeping, or maybe there is magic in the bones. The important thing is, Chief is alive, and..." the deer paused swinging his massive antlers and deep eyes around to stare at Destiny, "and he would like to go home... with you, if you'll let him?"

A cry tore from her lips, and the tears spilled down her face. "Yes," she cried, dropping to her knees and wrapping her arms lightly around the startled dog's neck. "I want to go home—with my family."

Caesar exhaled a long breath he hadn't known he was holding. "Home," he agreed.

"We can help you with that," White Cloud assured, nodding to Boulder and Goes Ahead who stepped forward.

Soon, goodbyes and thanks were said. Sam and Pete, declining their invitation to join on the other side, said they preferred to try out their next adventure as part of, in their words, 'the bison posse.'

River had waved his goodbye heading toward the ferry awaiting him at the river. The pheasant pair—

who had somehow survived the battle along with a smattering of chittering chipmunks, prairie dogs, and a lone antelope—having lost its fellows—decided they too would remain with the horses and bison. There were sure to be scattered coyotes and wolves nearby. Boulder vowed they'd be dealt with and driven from the prairie, as well as the lone mountain lion that most likely still prowled the area.

And so, after a long day of battle, two pomeranians, a human, a tortoise, and one revived Rez Dog found themselves secured atop horses, bison, and deer, headed toward the human zone entry, near the naturally beautiful rimrocks, all the while trailed by an extremely tired yet satisfied magpie.

EPILOGUE

"There's no way that happened!" Duke's ornery littermate—Rowen—interrupted.

I spluttered, snapping back to the present. I had lost myself in the storytelling and instead of the warm spring day in Mom's backyard, I had been off in the majesty of the wild Montana prairie chaperoned by the mighty bison, eagles, and deer.

"Be quiet!" Duke, the tiny chihuahua, whined. "I want to hear the end!"

Birds of all variety chittered in agreement. Even the silly P'jean and Maria, the dove pair, had become enraptured with the tortoise's tale.

"Why? None of that is real. It's just a stupid story from an old talking rock!" Rowen said snidely.

"Wow, does your mom know how you speak to your elders?" A woman's voice cut in, calmly yet authoritatively.

The puppy yelped as if it had been spanked.

I smiled inwardly, turning to see Destiny. She was older now, like me. Her dark long hair had gone gray, visible in her ponytail. Her tan, weathered face was lit by her sparkling, mischievous eyes. Being up there in years hadn't slowed her down, and she didn't hesitate to plop onto the grass to sit cross-legged next to me and the puppies on the other side of the fence.

"You speak 'dog?'" Duke asked, awed.

"Yes," she laughed. "I can speak to all animals," she looked pointedly at the mean puppy who sat with his ears drooping and tail between his legs, "a lasting remnant of my time in the animal zone."

A robin whistled at that!

Destiny pushed her flannel sleeve up to reveal perfect teeth marks dug into her forearm.

"From Samson the coyote," Duke breathed. And even his mean littermate couldn't argue. This was a talking human after all.

"Can you tell us what happened after? How does the story end?"

Destiny sighed, her eyes growing glassy as she ran a palm over my large, smooth shell. She smiled, "Would you like to tell, or shall I?"

I closed my eyes, enjoying the warmth from her palm as well as the late afternoon sun. "You tell it, sister, my throat has gone dry."

"Well, as you can imagine Mom and Dad weren't exactly pleased with us," she started, laughing at the memory, her voice sounding decades younger.

She was right. Mom and Dad were so relieved, happy... and furious with all of them. An interesting mixture, I recalled.

"When we got back, a doctor stitched my shoulder wounds—you should see those scars," she said, dryly. "And then we took Chief to the vet. He almost lost his leg... protecting me," she said, her voice growing distant.

"It was there, as I watched the vet stitch up my friend, still able to understand everything he and the other animals in the office were saying, I knew what I wanted to do with the rest of my life. I became a veterinarian," Destiny said proudly, adding, "An animal doctor."

The puppies nodded then, understanding.

"And Chief and I," she smiled, "We helped each other heal, as only two kids from the Rez could. Chief was my best friend. We understood each other and helped each other overcome our scars, finding our place in our family... and in the world."

She smiled, still rubbing my shell. I didn't take it personally. I could remember those days well. Destiny was forever changed after her run in with Razor and the coyotes. She was nicer. Happier. And so nurturing. She—and Empress—both took great care of Chief, who remained part of the family for the rest of his long life.

I picked up the tale, "Mom and Dad couldn't believe the change in Destiny. They adopted her the next year officially and kept Chief at her insistence. We lived as a family quite happily."

"I took Chief with me to college in Bozeman. And would bring him home most weekends and holiday/summer breaks. A couple of my professors even let me bring him to class." Destiny recalled.

I smiled recollecting. Mom and Dad would sometimes pile us in the car to go visit her as well.

"What happened to them?" The tiny chihuahua asked, innocently.

My heart panged, nonetheless.

Destiny sighed again. "Well, Caesar, my tiny hero, passed away at the old age of seventeen. I was an adult by then and came home just in time to say goodbye. And...," she cut off, licking her lips. "Empress, it seemed, couldn't imagine a life without her partner-in-crime. She passed quietly that night in her sleep."

Tears streaked down Destiny's face.

"I'm sorry," Duke whispered, tears filling his big puppy eyes. "I didn't mean to—"

"Oh, it's alright, little one," Destiny said, reaching her hand through the fence slats to scratch his ears. "It's good to remember," sniffing, and adding in a firmer voice, "they deserve to be remembered. Chief lived with me a few years more, and then he too passed away. I buried him back on the reservation. Empress and Caesar are buried on our old property in Molt."

I nodded along, having been there for all of it. My heart hurt with the memories.

"So," Destiny picked up, "in memory of them, I opened my own Veterinary Clinic, The Animal Zone."

Destiny dug out her phone, and swiped, before pushing it through the slats.

The chihuahua puppy pack leaned close, "Whoa," the largest puppy said.

"Is that you?" Duke asked.

"Yep, that's me... and that's Caesar, Empress, Pharaoh, and Chief."

"And... Enzo?" Duke asked, spying the bird perched in a tree in the background of the old photograph.

Destiny laughed, tears spilling down her cheeks. "And Enzo. That chattering bird lived out on our property for the rest of his life. I had this photo enlarged and it hangs still to this day in my," she paused, "in my former clinic."

She drew her phone back, explaining, "I recently retired. After Dad died last year, I closed the clinic to take care of Mom—and Pharaoh. We sold their home in Molt, and they moved in with me and my husband here." She explained, "Our kids are all grown and live in Western Montana and Idaho. I want to travel and see my grandkids, and not be so tied to work. I still help at a horse stable from time to time and will never completely be without animal friends. I even," she paused for effect, "helped deliver you."

"You did?" Duke asked.

"Yep, you were the runt."

"Yeah, I know," Duke murmured, ignoring his littermates' snickering.

"Ya know… I always had a soft spot for runts. And so…," she paused, eyeing me.

Something in her voice seemed off. "What is it, Destiny?" I asked.

"Well, I thought it might be nice to have a new face around here," she smiled widely, the skin near her eyes crinkling merrily as she leaned toward the fence. "How would you like to come live with us, Duke?"

The tiny puppy's jaw almost hit the grass. "Do you mean it?" He squeaked, his ears flopping adorably as he quivered with excitement.

"I mean it," Destiny said. "I've already spoken to your owner—and your mother," nodding her head toward the chihuahua matriarch who had just walked out into the yard. "You'll still be able to see your mom and littermates anytime, but you can come live with us. It would be nice to have another tiny tail around."

"Wow," was all Duke could say. His littermates looking at him as if suddenly seeing him for the first time.

Later that night, Duke snuggled into his bed beside me who lay next to a rocking chair, where Mom sat. Davina smiled warmly.

"Here's your tea, Mom," Destiny said, handing a steaming teacup to her mother—topping off the gesture with a kiss on the cheek. She then plopped down on the ground to scratch behind Duke's ears.

"Well," the old woman began, "is anyone up for a story? I thought of one young Duke might like. How about the story of the famous Duke of Suffolk who became the best friend to a King?"

Destiny looked at me, as we shared a smile. Being retired had never stopped Mom from telling her historical tales. I was glad for it. Mom and Destiny seemed only too happy to have a youngster in the home again. It would be good for all of them.

As the fireplace crackled, and Mom in her soft, melodic voice began, Duke's eyes grew droopy. I closed my eyes, soaking in the peaceful moment, but before I drifted off to sleep, I heard Destiny whisper.

"Goodnight, Duke. Welcome to the family... and to your forever home."

Acknowledgments:

As always starting a new project is exciting and scary. Being known for writing my earlier series (*Nav'Aria*), made me really question this one. "I'm a fantasy writer, what am I doing writing a Middle Grade book?" I'm glad I didn't let the self-doubt hold me back. I was inspired to write this one (as I share in my Author Note) and I'm so grateful for my wonderful team who helps me get my words down... and share them!

I couldn't do any of this without my fantastic editor, Heather Peers. Thank you from the bottom of my heart, Heather. You were the first person to believe in *Nav'Aria* (besides family) and to have your help and support on another project means the world to me. You're a true friend. (And thanks for not throwing the *Tiny Tails* draft away when you thought the ending was crap.) *The copy she first received was missing the final twenty pages. Oops!!! That would've been a very lame cliffhanger.*

Thank you to my team of beta readers, Diana, Keil, Jarica, Kaitlin, and Jessica for your instant connection with *The Legend of Tiny Tails.* Your enthusiasm really made me excited to share this one.

Thank you SO MUCH to my formatter (and husband), Keil Backer. Your keen eye and diligence are incredibly helpful and allowed for *Tiny Tails* to be presented in such a gorgeous way. I know readers (whether they realize it or not) will appreciate all the hours you poured into making sure each page is aligned, the fonts match, and the overall placement of headings, etc. made for a pleasant reading experience. It's something that many of us take for granted when reading a book… and that's when you know it was done well. Thanks for always being the best support system ever.

Thank you to the insanely talented Josh Wirth, cover artist extraordinaire (and photographer). Josh, this cover is PERFECT. I love what you came up with and am honored to have your art coupled with mine. I think we created something very cool, and I'm excited for kids to explore *The Legend of Tiny Tails*, daydreaming of owls, tiny dogs, and the Montana prairie enhanced by your illustrations. I also love the interior paw prints! Thanks for everything!

A huge THANK YOU to my proofreader (and bro/best friend), Dave Jones. You're the kindest, smartest guy around, and the best person for this job. I trust your "teacher eye." Bust out the red pen! I appreciate you! It felt really good to have another pair of eyes on this book before release.

I'm so grateful for my readers, and my wonderful friends online (Instagram, Facebook, and Twitter) who continually support and cheer me on.

I'm truly blessed to have the most EPIC family/hype squad ever. (Love you guys!) **I want to give a special shoutout to my mom, Diana, who encouraged me to release this book into the world.** She was the first person to read this one, and being a dog mom herself, fell in love with Caesar and the gang. Thank you, mom, for always being there for me. For supporting me. And for being the sweetest, most loving grandma ever.

AUTHOR'S NOTE:

What a crazy couple of years, #amiright!?

During the COVID-19 pandemic, I was asked to return to teaching for the 2020-2021 school year. It was an interesting time to go from working at home to returning to the classroom, while many other people I knew were being sent home to work remote. I tried to make the most of it and soaked up the wonderful time with my students. It wasn't their fault any of this was happening.

They experienced the loss of school events, sports, dances, field trips, and so many other activities, as well as more serious issues like dealing with the loss of a loved one, health scares, parent's splitting up, and/or parent's struggling financially throughout the pandemic.

While I'm grateful we were in an area that had schools stay open for much of the pandemic (with the option to go remote), the students still had to deal with contact-tracing, social distancing, masks, a tense political/election season, etc.

With all of that in mind, I really tried to bring energy and passion every day to enliven and enrich our history lessons. One way I found that made the teens smile, was to tell them funny anecdotes about my pets. I have two pomeranians, a tortoise, and a chihuahua puppy... (who yes, along with my adopted daughter, inspired this very story). I would show pictures and tell funny puppy stories to start our class. If I forgot, the students would ask me for pictures or more stories. With so much stress and uncertainty around, a few minutes chatting animal antics was a sweet reprieve for the kids and myself. It carried on this way for months, and by January 2021, I began to tell them of the other animals I encountered too.

The morning after we brought our chihuahua puppy home (Dec. 27th, 2020), I let him out to go potty and saw a GIANT OWL SITTING ON MY NEIGHBOR'S ROOF. It watched the little puppy, who was as tiny as a mouse! Totally freaked me out. I ran around clapping and shouting like a crazy person (probably drove my neighbors nuts) so it would go away and not make a meal out of my little buddy. I haven't seen it around since, but I can hear two owls every night nearby our home in Eastern Montana. So, my family knows my strict instructions: No puppies go outside without a human attendant, and a flashlight!

The first Monday after winter break, I was planning to tell my students all about my new puppy, and the owl sighting. But on the way to school, I saw a HUGE bald eagle sitting in a tree. That day I told my students lots of animal stories (and some history stuff too). But then I saw the eagle the next day. And another one, in a different part of town, the next day. And the next. And one flew over our school when I was walking in the parking lot. I saw Bald Eagles for at least eight days in a row. Now, maybe you're a lucky person and you see them all the time... I have lived in Montana for over twenty-years now and have never seen that many eagles!

It got me thinking about owls and eagles. I looked up the symbolism and found that in many indigenous cultures and stories owls are viewed as dark, evil, or a sign of death while eagles are viewed as hopeful or pure. Throw in a couple sightings of the albino deer that lives near my house, and suddenly *The Legend of Tiny Tails* appeared in my head! I told my students bits here and there and once the school year wrapped up; I wrote *this* story.

My silver lining throughout the pandemic was teaching. I was called a couple days before school, and for some reason said *yes* to taking the position. I think it's because I needed those kids, and I like to think, they enjoyed their time in Mrs. Backer's class. It was in that room that *Tiny Tails* was born. So, while I'm relieved and hopeful to move away from the COVID years, I'll forever treasure my time in 2020-2021 filled with kids, pet talk, and a whole bunch of owls and eagles. This book is for my students... and for you.

Whatever you're going through, I hope you remember that you are capable of so much. Just like Caesar, Destiny, Pharaoh, Empress, and Chief. You can overcome a whole lotta stuff, especially when you find some great people (or animals) to cheer you on. Be kind. Be brave. And never give up. At the end of the day, don't forget to look up, my darling readers. There are eagles all around!

May you always: Dream BIG. Be EPIC. And SHINE on.

~K.J.

Thanks so much for reading *The Legend of Tiny Tails*. If you enjoyed the story, please let me know!

Reviews are incredibly helpful. And if you're a teacher or work in a school and would like for me to come speak with your students, please get in touch. (K.J. Backer on all social media). Visit **https://kjbacker.com** to learn more and to sign up for my newsletter! I may just have another pet adventure or two up my sleeve! And for the adult readers, or when you kids get a bit older, check out *Nav'Aria* my adult fantasy series.

***

It is my dream that every child and pet will have a loving, forever home. I believe that starts with us. When you say *yes* to bringing home a child and/or pet, make sure you really do mean forever. Children—and our pets—are not temporary. Love and cherish them... and commit to them. Those bonds are special and meant to last.

I share more about our family's adoption story on social media and on my website blog. We are blessed to have our daughter who we adopted at the age of nine.

We are also extremely obsessed with and dedicated to our pets. And while I may not speak 'dog,' I do think we have a special connection. Caesar and the gang were hugely inspired by my little ones.

Made in USA - North Chelmsford, MA
1332162_9781732920668
09.13.2022 1632